THE TAKING DOWN OF A
CRIMINAL EMPIRE

Other novels by the same Author

The Sterling Connection

The Rand Connection

The Ruble Connection

The DC Connection

New Directions

All of the above novels are based on the Main Character Paul Blair, retired Civil Engineer, and former Special Forces Officer.

Blood under the Maple Leaf

The Dawson Affair

Evil in Command

The First Nations Incident

The Taking Down of a Criminal Empire

The above novels have been based on Steve Benson an RCMP CID senior officer, and his small team of dedicated dedectives.

****

"My life it's been a hell of a ride," (A short autobiography of the Author WJ Adair Pen Name 'Liam Adair')

THE TAKING DOWN OF A
CRIMINAL EMPIRE

Liam Adair

ISBN: Softcover   978-1-7960-0191-4
              eBook   978-1-7960-0190-7

Print information available on the last page.

Rev. date: 05/22/2019

To order additional copies of this book, contact:
Xlibris
1-800-455-039
www.Xlibris.com.au
Orders@Xlibris.com.au
722235

CHAPTER 1

OTTAWA SUN
June 7th 2016
Senior Crime Reporter; - Jack Watson

"On location in the Aylmer Lake district of the Northwest Territories. The remains Of two bodies of a young male and female have discovered by a party of campers about 18 kilometers south of Aylmer Lake. As it happens, I was on a family camping trip to the area. The area where the remains were found was off the beaten track, North of Reliance in the Northwest Territories, and would have gone undiscovered for a very long time. The difficulty was access to this section of the wilderness for the police conducting an in-depth investigation, as the small city of Reliance is the nearest point to civilisation."

"There are indications that the pair were brutally murdered due to a large number of blunt force trauma, found on the skeletal remains. At this point, police have said that it may take some time to identify these remains. Police have also informed me that they will make a long and exhaustive study of DNA taken from family members who reported the couple missing at the time of their disappearance. Therefore, no actual details have been released. One police source told me that identification might only be possible using DNA, but after such a long time it is not guaranteed as being a surety."

****

1

It was time to get down to some serious work now that DS Jerry Armstrong was back on deck, after his honeymoon. It would take Jerry several days to unravel the various typed and hadwritten notes the team had waiting for him to support. "I can see you've made a mess but not achieved a lot," was Armstrong's comment. He was only partially successful ducking award of missiles thrown in his direction harmony has been restored Steve Benson thought, he sat there thinking, as a Detective Chief superintendent, and leader of this small group of very dedicated detectives.

The team being Detective Chief Superintended Steve Benson, (team leader,) Detective Inspector Al Philips his 2IC, Detective Sergeant Jimmy Two Bears (First Nations tribal Chief), Detective Sergeant Jill Burrows, Detective Sergeant Jerry Armstrong (their computer whiz and IT expert). Dr. Donna Connors a foremost Forensic Pathologist. A small but very committed team.

Mr. Collins QC the senior prosecutor for the Attorney General, gave Steve a report on how well Al Philips and Jimmy Two Bears, had held their own against the legal profession when the last combined criminal cases proceeded through the court system. It made Steve proud that he may just have played a small part in their coming of age. Steve sat in the squad room thanking after all the difficulties I believe I have created something of value that will last the years to come. He thought nothing succeeds like success, and it will have its rewards. Now Jerry has returned it was back to the humdrum of choosing the next case/cases to solve.

"Jerry I want you to catch up with his team's notes when you are not working on these two particular cases. As well Jerry try to get hold of Donna to have a look at the forensic reports. Do not forget to tell her it's another open unsolved and the crime very likely took place it in a remote area of the Northwest Territories." Steve knew he did not have to look or Jerry's shoulder to check.

"Donna will be here in 30 minutes or so boss," Jerry told Steve a few moments later.

Jerry had already rearranged the possible list of cases to tackle. Steve had had the team do an in-depth study of the cases listed which he had extracted from the unsolved list he had first suggested. Steve's only worry was keeping everyone's feet on the ground and focused on the task. Steve was well aware by bringing the First Nations Incident to a satisfactory conclusion had been no easy task.

OTTAWA SUN,
June 25th 2016
Senior Crime Reporter, 'Jack Watson'

"This report concerns the fact from an inside source of the disappearance of an elected Member of Parliament, Gregory Stains. Government sources were attempting to keep a lid on this. Stains disappeared on an official visit to the Northwest Territories, as the Junior Member, Assistant, to the Minister for First Nations. The whereabouts of Stains was not known at the time of his disappearance. The Prime Mister put a 'DNotice' on the case until police authorities had time to investigate the situation."

"There was considerable tension at the time between the local First Nations tribe's ad Prospectors regarding prospecting for rare minerals, on land designated belonging to First Nations. The primary purpose of Stains' visit was to investigate the fact that precious metals were being mined I an area, which under the law was the property of First Nations. Gold and diamonds had already been found in several places, and the number of claims disputes had increased accordingly with the rising number of mining claims registered with the Department of Mines.

There were two cases suggested for study, one by Al Philips and the other by Jerry Armstrong. One from a Detective's point of view, and one from a computer analysts point of view. The two cases picked out also had newspaper reports attached all of which Jerry had sent to Steve's computer. Steve sat there going over these statements while the rest made some sense of the original investigation of the death of a newly married young couple conducted and abandoned when the case had been declared open/unsolved. On the surface, they both looked to be difficult and would need a lot of hard work, but that was the point of the exercise

From the files Jerry had extracted the names and rank of the senior investigators a DCI Alex Henderson and a DI Phil Hughes.

Standing in front of the newly cleaned whiteboards and waiting till the room had settled before starting, Steve said, "We came out smelling of roses, last run-in with the legal profession, but don't let that go to your head. The trouble is we have set the bar very high now, and if we are not careful, we will hang ourselves with our own hype. When we get around to questioning the lead investigators outtakes the DCI, and just for a change, Jimmy can have the DI. If Jimmy gets into trouble you can take over Al."

"In spite of all that I say, let the games begin." Steve said as he stood there. "The most important thing you and that is all of you should have learned from the first nations incident is, at a certain amount of lateral thinking may need to be applied to solving any case not forgetting the old standby of real police legwork, tiresome as it may be." Do not let the case or who it involves distract you from the core facts of the case itself. I am happy you stuck with it. There was a time when I did think it would be my swansong. Thanks to you I live to fight another day."

Steve thought he could have enjoyed retirement. He did not have any outstanding debts and had enough money in the bank to live in relative comfort. The hard part would be not having a positive direction to help keep his feet planted.

I came to welcome Jerry back into the fold the CC also extends his good wishes."

"With tongue in cheek, I ask, does this mean Sir; our hard and mostly unrewarded efforts have made you look good to the CC." Steve wanted to know.

"Because having now earned yourselves so many brownie points, for your efforts, I will ignore that comment DCS. I will leave you now to let you get on with it."

A few minutes after the AC left, "I suppose I better try and make peace with the AC," Steve said as he went towards his office. Once seated he picked up his phone and dialled the AC's office. "Benson here Sir, I apologise for my earlier remarks, no offence intended. I did not get to ask you if you do any more odd cases floating around. I'm about to start reviewing the cold case file now that Jerry has sorted all the team reports into the system?"

"No offence taken. Unfortunately, I do not have any cases up my sleeve. However, none the less, the whole of the police system will have access to your computer files; maybe the rest might learn something. I will make sure that access is 'read only', so they cannot tread all over it with their size 12s."

"I have to warn you that I had Jerry put a super lock on the system to stop anyone getting into and altering any of the files. I also had Jerry do a separate computer backup in case of a malfunction."

"Very wise Steve, whatever, I have nothing for you. With all checks and balances in place have Jerry call me about this subject?"

"Okay chief. I will let you know what cases we decide to unravel."

"Do that," the AC said and broke the connection.

Steve made his way back to the central office. "Alright you geniuses what cases have you decided to tackle first?"

It was at that point that Doctor Donna Connors their pathologist came in with a cheery good morning and gave Jerry a big hug to welcome him back into the fold.

Then AI spoke up. "I have shortlisted two possibilities. The first being the death of a junior politician named Gregory Stains. He had been a politician for only three years but had been bright enough to get himself appointed to a seat on his party's Cabinet, and therefore there was a certain amount of initial panic when he disappeared. According to the parliamentary notice, Stains went to the Territories on a trip around his constituents. One of his functions was assistant to the Minister for Aboriginal Affairs, so this particular trip was a fact-finding mission.

According to the parliamentary file, this was a scheduled visit, so there should have been nothing out of the ordinary. Unfortunately, Stains went off the air, and not even his remains had been located to date. Assuming he had been murdered and not gone missing deliberately. It had also been reported that one of the people he met with at the time Tom Reynolds, a local small businessperson, also disappeared just over a month later. The two facts may be unrelated. I would still flag them as linked together. When Reynolds disappeared, it was still too soon after the disappearance of S therefore the two events had to be tied together."

"It is the fact that Reynolds also disappeared in an area which Stains had visited, that both disappearances had to be linked to each other. So if possible, Steve needed two things if they could be had, that is the reason they met and the place where the meeting occurred. Also a scheduled of Stains schedule of his visit to the Northwest Territories that was lodged with the Cabinet secretary before he left.

Steve went to the front of the whiteboards again. When he had their attention he said, "Jerry I want you to talk to the secretary of the parliamentary office that Stains was attached to at the time, and try to get some idea from the legislative records of Stains itinerary on the fateful trip. See if you can unearth the possible connection between Stains and Reynolds, outside of the usual business commitments. Al, Jill, and Jimmy, you start doing a breakdown of the investigation into the death of the young couple. Donna if you could do your study of the forensic reports such as they are and try and give us some direction."

CHAPTER 2

The second case put up the investigation was the murder of a newly married young couple whose remains had just been found. A party of campers about 18 km South of Aylmer Lake discovered the remains of the two bodies of a young male and female. The area where the remains were found was off the beaten track and they would have gone undiscovered for a very long time. The difficulty was access to this section of the wilderness for police doing an in-depth investigation, as Reliance is the nearest point to civilisation, and with only a small company of RCMP officers in resident.

There are indications that the pair were brutally murdered due to a large number of blunt force trauma found on the skeletal remains. The original police report states that it will take a long and exhaustive study of DNA taken from family members who reported the couple missing at the time of their disappearance. Therefore police believe that it will take longer to find out what happened or find out who killed this young couple if DNA was all they had to go by.

The couple who were enjoying the wilderness on their honeymoon had chosen the wilderness trip as something different. The couple in question had a permanent home in Edmonton, Alberta. They have now been identified as Sean and Sally Adams. They apparently had well-paid steady employment with no reference to them in police criminal files. Steve thought about it but had not broached the idea of mistaken identity; he would do it when he talked to Edmonton?

"Jerry try to get the senior RCMP officer in Edmonton on the phone, but before you connect me, make sure of the gender and rank of the Commandant so I don't say the wrong thing. I'll go into my office and wait till you connect me."

At the same time, Donna sat in one of the small rooms reading the forensic reports on both cases. She sat there thinking that there is not going be any direction to come from the DNA reports, and DNA would have only been a backup anyway. Donna thought I might in fact, have to go and cover the same ground where the young couple's remains were found to see if anything useful was not left behind. To do that I need Jimmy Two Bears because he was so very good at reading sign. She went out into the main room to talk to Steve. Jerry told her that Steve was in his office talking to the Commandant in Edmonton. "Donna can you wait until Steve has finished?"

When Steve picked up his phone having been warned by Jerry, he said, "DCS Benson speaking Ma'am, from the cold case squad in Ottawa."

"Good morning DCS what can I do for you?"

"I have reopened the case of the young couple whose remains have just been discovered in the Northwest Territories South of Aylmer Lake. They had a home in Edmonton, so I was curious to know if you conducted an area canvas around their home address, and if so what was the result?"

"I do not think it turned up much, but I will have you transferred to the DCI who was in charge."

There were a couple of clicks before a male voice said, "DCI Brian Forbes."

Steve introduced himself gave a quick explanation of what he needed. Forbes told him, that apart from confirming their identity they did not get much more from the house canvas. This couple had only small credit amounts outstanding. In other words, you average law-abiding citizens. The couple did not as far as could be ascertained have any connection to underworld crime figures. The DCI did not think it could have been a case of mistaken identity, but had no way to prove or disprove this theory.

Having said that, Steve gave the DCI his number and asked that he be contacted immediately if Edmonton made any breakthroughs.

When Steve came out of his office Donna said, "I believe that the way to move forward is to do a foot search of the area with old eagle eyes Jimmy, to see if we can up something that could have been missed. What do you think about that Jimmy?"

"Whatever gives us a start I'll be in it," Jimmy told them.

"Jill," Steve said, "How would you like a trip to the north-west for a bit of adventure?"

"I would love to be in that," Jill told Steve.

"You have been certified with a long gun, have you not Jill?"

"Yes boss."

"That means Jimmy, that with yours and Jill's issue side arms you will have five guns. Okay, Donna when can you leave?"

"As soon as everybody is ready," Donna told him.

"As it is Wednesday, how about tomorrow or even today. Jerry see what is available for transport and accommodation for three. Jimmy, I want you to draw out two long guns want you and Jill. What have you got in the way of small arms, Donna?"

"I have just been issued with a Glock 19.9 semiautomatic which holds 15 rounds and is extremely lightweight, I have been certified on the firing range for the use of this pistol," Donna told Steve.

That settles it Jimmy, you can draw the long guns and extra ammo before you go."

Jerry cut in saying he had three seats available for a flight to Yellowknife, with a helicopter standing by to take them into the search area.

"Okay, Jerry check the weather condition. Jimmy, you are the expert decide what outdoor clothing you require and draw them from the quartermaster. Last but not least a long-range two-way radio for communication. When everybody is happy with the arrangements booked the flights Jerry."

"Already done boss."

The trio went to the QM store to be issued with the outdoor clothing Jimmy suggested and a small very powerful easily portable radio. Then they went to the armoury to draw out their weapons and extra ammo. Then being equipped for bear, they were ready to leave.

Steve accompanied them to the airport with the usual warnings about keeping their heads down and following gems Jimmy's directions if the weather closed in. Steve told them to take the time, especially as they had plenty of that now. Lastly, he said to them that he would make sure they had plenty of backup from Yellowknife.

When he got back to the office, Steve called Yellowknife base to warn them and to ensure that whatever assistance the trio might require was extended to them. He also wanted to make sure that the trio had access to snowmobiles and dog sleigh teams, and most importantly tents and sleeping bags.

When the trio arrived in Yellowknife, they were picked up by a couple of constables in a small bus and taken to the barracks. The Commandant was there to greet them. Jimmy asked the CO if he could have two additional troopers as a backup. As Jimmy told the CO, they would need to have had extreme weather training and be well versed in the use of a long gun.

"I have just the two for this job. A Corporal Barry Gibbs who has spent a lot of time in and around the Arctic circle and more importantly is a crack shot with a long gun, and trooper Jack Forbes, who has also spent a lot of time in remote areas.

"If you would let me have them, it means we can take two more snowmobiles and trailers."

"I will have them standing by at the QM's store." The Commandant told them.

At the QM's store, introductions were made all around. Gibbs looked to be very fit, with a demeanour that suggested he could hadle himself regardless of the situation. Forbes was a grizzled old-timer who looked like he had just stepped out of a page of the RCMP history book.

"I remember now corporal; you were on one of the survival courses I conducted at the Academy?" Jimmy asked while he shook hads with trooper Forbes.

"That's correct Sir."

"No need to call me Sir, boss will do. Now let's get on with this." Jimmy then stood by while the equipment was sorted and loaded onto the trailers. It only took a short time, and everything was ready to go. It was now time to head for a meal, after which as the day was running out, they went to their allotted accommodation for a good night's sleep so that they could set out early the next morning.

By 10 o'clock mid-morning they were on site. The chopper was big enough to carry the other snowmobiles and two trailers and some extra fuel packed aboard one of them. One of the officers who had come with them showed Jimmy where the remains were found. As it was a bright cloudless day Jimmy picked out a campsite, and with extra hads, the camp was set up in no time.

Jimmy and his little band said goodbye and the helicopter was off back to base. The first thing Jimmy did as soon as the helicopter left was a radio check everything was fine. Satisfied he got a fire and coffee going so he could talk to the two girls.

"If the weather turns bad we will need to be in one tent. More importantly, we will need to be in the same sleeping bag. If that is necessary, we will sipper two sleeping bags together. So get over your inhibitions if it becomes a matter of survival. Okay ladies? One of you will be with me and the other with Barry or Jack or you can cut me out and I'll bunk with whoever whoever is left."

They both knew and understood so there should be no problems.

When had finished their coffee, Jimmy took them to a starting point from where they could examine the area. He put sticks to Mark the start and every time they changed direction. The routine over the next two days became fixed, but they none the less managed to cover a 10 sq km section. Anything they found was left in place and flagged with a marker, which Jimmy noted on a map of the area using his portable compass.

Jimmy made sure they carried their firearms with them at all times. Jill kept thinking that Jimmy was so methodical the way he went about everything. She didn't feel intimidated by her surroundings and the fact they were in a wilderness area, when you had Jimmy Two Bears in charge. It was also the way Jimmy insisted that they leave behind no rubbish.

The problem was that they were in that area of the Northwest Territories, which had yielded gold strikes and better still, diamonds. Already tall tales were doing the rounds about fallouts between prospectors about which one had the legitimate rights to whatever was found.

At the end of the third day, Jimmy told the other four that they would spend the next morning collecting anything that had been discovered. What appeared to be relevant they would pick up, but leave the marker and anything else not relevant in-situ. They would take away what had already been collected, and regardless they would leave all the tags in place for further reference.

Jimmy made sure they carried their firearms with at all times. Jill kept thinking that Jimmy was so methodical the way he went about everything. She didn't feel intimidated by her surroundings and the fact that they were in a wilderness area, having Jimmy Two Bears in charge. It was also the way Jimmy insisted that they leave no rubbish behind.

The problem was that they were in that area of the Northwest Territories that had yielded Gold strikes and better still, Diamonds. Already tall tales were doing the rounds about fallouts between prospectors about who had the legitimiate rights to whatever was found.

At the end of the third day, Jimmy told the other four that they would spend the next morning collecting anything that had been discovered, what appeared to be relevant they would pick-up, but leave the marker in-situ. They would take what they had already collected, and regardless they would leave all markers in place for futher reference.

About late morning Jimmy will was thinking of calling a lunch break when he had the sensation of being watched. All five were sitting on logs in a slight hollow when Jimmy said quietly," I want you two ladies to keep on talking about some of the articles we have found so far, and try and get a little friendly argument going. I have the feeling we are being watched."

"Barry and I will slide out like a couple of shadows to check our surroundings, and I want you Jack to guard the camp." The girls nodded their understanding and kept on talking, but both put their firearms in a position already cocked so no time would be wasted cocking and loading their guns.

Jimmy and Barry slipped away like wafers of mist, one left one right, to do a recce of the area, while the girls kept up the pretence of an argument over what had been found. Barry came across two men who looked liked they had the camp under surveillance. He gave a birdcall that he knew Jimmy would respond to while keeping a strict watch on the two men.

Jimmy sidled up to Barry and made a gesture for Barry to come in behind the man on the left while Jimmy came up behind the man on the right. IN a voice that sounded like it came from the grave, Jimmy said, "Put your weapons down slowly and raise your hads."

The one that Barry was covering decided to take his chances and swung his rifle towards Jimmy's position just as Barry cold-cocked him with the butt of his gun. The other one just put down his weapon and raised his in a gesture of surrender. Jimmy quickly frisked the man to find he also had two hadguns a large hunting knife and extra ammunition. Once he was relieved of the additional weaponry, Jimmy put his hads behind his back before slipping on two cable ties, and another couple of cable ties around his ankles.

Barry had done the same to the other man.

"Okay, let's see if we can't get some information from this rat who are you and why are you here," Jimmy asked the man. With no answer forthcoming, Jimmy fired a round from his revolver close to man's ear.

The man stayed silence showing he would not be an easy nut to crack.

Jimmy fired his gun again just nicking the man's ear, who without hesitation yelled, and started to blubber.

Once they had some idea of what these two were up to Jimmy Said, "That's it, Barry you head for the camp. Make sure they are in an area that they can defend and bring back a snowmobile and trailer so we can take these two back to base."

Barry was back in no time. He and Jimmy picked up the two would be assassins and dumped in the trailer. Jimmy made sure the two men were out of earshot before making the radio call to Yellowknife. With the senior officer on the line, Jimmy gave a quick explanation and the fact that he wanted the two would be assassins airlifted back to Yellowknife for interviewing and charging if necessary. The chopper was there within the hour with extra hads to escort the prisoners back to Yellowknife. A senior officer also came to make sure Jimmy and his small squad were not under threat of any kind. Satisfied he left promising Jimmy to let him know if any usable intelligence was the outcome.

This incident called for a change in strategy. Jimmy held a group meeting in one of the tents. When he had their attention Jimmy said, "To start with we are in a position that is not easily defended. The people who sent these two to spy on us should be already wondering why they haven't reported in. I want to do a quick pick up of any items we are taking back with us. I want a trooper to standby to keep the campsite under guard but I want you to do it from an undercover position outside the camp area. The rest of us will go out and do any other pickups required. We will spend the night here and head back to Yellowknife in the morning." Jimmy made a guard roster for the night. He did not think any bad people would attack the camp tonight; still, he was not going to make it easy for them.

Everybody was up at first light. The two girls got breakfast going, while the men started packing up the trailers with the tents and equipment. It took about an hour and a half and there were on their way South. In spite of snow falling, they made good time. Jimmy intended to keep going as long as he could before calling a halt for a meal break.

One of the local troopers pointed out the fact that they were almost in Reliance. We must be making good time Jimmy thought. "We may as well keep going to a point on the top end of the Great Lake, before heading on to Yellowknife." Jimmy told them.

It only took a couple of hours more travel to find a small cabin used by hunters. They moved straight in and made themselves to home. There was plenty of room for the five of them. So they set themselves up for the night. Between them, they had a fire going and a meal cooking. Jimmy was glad they were off the trail with a roof over their heads. Jimmy called Jerry back at base to report their current position and the fact that everyone was in good health.

After a good night's rest and a hearty breakfast, they were off to Yellowknife. The trail was easy going, so with one meal break and one coffee break they were in the area of Yellowknife by late afternoon. At the base, Jimmy left the rest to unpack and return their snowmobiles, trailers, and equipment while he reported to the Commandant.

The RCMP chief listened until Jimmy was finished before asking any pertinent questions. The senior officer had Jimmy's report taped ready for hard copies to be made. "That was an excellent report DS Two Bears; you are a credit to your current boss DCS Benson. You can stand down for now and relax," he told Jimmy.

CHAPTER 3

On the morning the trio Jill, Donna, and Jimmy arrived at their search area. Steve was just drawing up a plan to organise a neighbourhood search to try to find out where Gregory Stains the politician had gone missing.

Jerry was still waiting for the Parliamentary Secretary to supply him with the itinerary of Stains' visit to the Northwest Territories. Jerry was about to make another request when the route was posted to his electronic meal system. Now they had a starting point. The trouble for the team might be the fact that Stains visit was several hundred kilometres from where Jerry and the two girls were operating. This meant that the team would be spread over a significant portion of the Northwest Territories. Steve knew he would have to rely on the good graces of the AC for more help if it became necessary. However Steve was confident that if it meant more significant unsolved cases cleared off the books, that the AC would give Steve any additional aid he needed.

After a quick study of Stains' itinerary, Jerry passed it over to Steve. Steve also had a good look before giving it to Al Philips his 2IC. Stains' agenda did not live any time wasting, so he would have been busy up to the time he disappeared. The purpose of Stains' visit was to sort out some problems the local First Nations were having regarding boundary lines and prospecting. Stains had elected to be based mainly in Wrigley, on the Mackenzie River.

The RCMP station at Wrigley consisted of only two persons. Steve intended that with the A/C is applying two, he could set up a larger base in Wrigley. Steve did not want to waste anymore time, so he picked up his phone and called the A/C. When the AC answered, Steve said, "Benson again Sir. I have decided to and close the file on the missing Parliamentarian Gregory Stains. I would like to make a trip to Wrigley, which has only on the two troopers at any time. Therefore, I would like to borrow at least two troopers from here. Is that is a goal, I will pick them because they need also need to have had extended experience in in the Arctic Circle. If we include two from here it is better than bringing troopers in from all over the place."

"That seems reasonable Steve. Why not take four. I will instruct the local commander to expect you and be ready to transfer four troopers on a temporary basis to you."

"Thank you, Sir, Benson out."

Okay Al you come with me to the local barracks to help pick four troopers for temporary attachment to this squad. They must be well versed with surviving in the Arctic Circle; they will also need to be good riflemen. We might as well go now. You're in charge for the moment Jerry," Steve said as he went out the door.

Jerry thought, how is you only leave me in charge when there is no one to be in charge of.

Steve and Al left for the short trip to the barracks. On arrival, they were escorted to the office of the Commandant Bill Paxton. After introductions, the local chief said, "I was looking forward to meeting you DCS Benson." Steve then gave the commander a quick précis of the case.

"After which the commander said follow me this way this way. I have six men standing by for you to interview now." The men were assembled in the common room and came to attention when their chief arrived with his two visitors. "You all know the purpose of this gathering, so I'm going to leave you in the capable hads of DCS Benson." On that note, the commander took his leave after he gave the personnel files of the men to Steve. Present there was a Sergeant two Corporals and three Troopers.

"First I am DCS Steve Benson, and this is DI Alan Philips. This exercise is for a special assignment to Wrigley just south of the Arctic Circle. Now have you all had experience of the frozen North?"

There was a chorus of, "Yes Sir."

"Now have any of you got an up and coming event such as childbirth, family emergency, that would exclude you from this assignment, or anything that would take your mind off the job?"

One man put up his had to say his wife was expected to go into labour in about a month's time.

"I would hope that this affair is over by then. I will exclude you for now, but standby I may be able to put you to use in some other capacity. Take a note of that Al. Now anybody else?" With no takers Steve continued, "AI can you had out those notes we put together."

As Steve was speaking, his 2IC passed out a one-page list of notes about what the case involved. As they discussed the situation amongst themselves, Steve called the Sergeant order him.

"Sir, what can I do for you," The Sergeant asked politely.

"Now let's get this off to a good start. You can call me boss like the rest of my squad. I would like you along on this adventure as the local voice of authority. I have command permission to pick four of you, assuming you are coming who else would you suggest?"

"Right boss," Stephens replied with more enthusiasm. "Jim Henry for one. Joe Bascal, I have already made one trip North with him a good man when the chips are down. The third one would be Jack Evans; he has done quite a bit of time in the area north of the Circle."

"Call them forward in the following order, Evans, Henry and Bascal. Remember this exercise involves a politician, so there will be the inevitable politics brought into this. Therefore, everyone has to keep that in mind. Now before we start do you think any of them have open political sentiments?"

"No boss, I don't think so."

"I want you to bring up that point when you do the interviews with the DI overlooking your shoulder, while I sit back and observe are you happy with that?"

"Yes, boss."

"Okay let's get this show on the road," Steve told them.

Each interview lasted about 15 minutes. Before each man was dismissed, Al waited for the nod from Steve every time. As it happened, Steve was happy to go with the Sergeant's choice.

"Now," Steve wanted to know, "how many of you have taken the survival course at the? You should be happy to know that one of the instructors is a permanent member of the squad."

In fact, all six had passed the course.

First, he warned them they were clear on temporary assignment to Wrigley that fact is not to be disclosed to anyone outside this group. Now he had picked those to go, that left two the expectant husband and another trooper. Steve announced who would be one of the team, but he told the other two that were not going to remain here for the present. He then outlined what he thought would be the way the investigation would be conducted." Solve the first order of the day is to draw what equipment we can from the QM's store and assemble it ready to transport to Wrigley. I would like you to organise that Sergeant," Steve told Stephens.

With everyone kitted out they were more or less ready for the. That was when Steve got the disturbing news from Jimmy near Aylmer Lake.

"Hold on Jimmy," Steve said while he passed on the information to Al about the two men Jimmy had caught watching what Jimmy and the rest were doing up there.

"Jimmy I want you to keep heading south. I will talk to Yellowknife now to make sure they can execute an emergency pickup if necessary. You know the drill, be safe." Benson listening out.

To Al, Steve said, "anyone else leading that little band I might worry, but have a start wary about Jimmy, it will definitely be time to retire. I'm going to have a word with Yellowknife using the radio from here.

When Steve had Yellowknife on air, he asked for the CO. There was no time wasted before the CO came on air. The Benson Sir. I want to waste time recalling the events regarding Aylmer Lake. You would be more aware of the situation regarding my people doing an investigation in that area. I have every confidence that DS Two Bears will have it under control. Nonetheless I would like you to put in place an emergency evacuation should it become necessary, as my people have already discovered they were under surveillance."

"The bad guys like a concerted attack, DS two bears will be able to hold off, depending on the strength of the attack until you send help. He will set up a camp perimeter that lets him guard all. Can you have an operator listen out for the new DS Jimmy Two Bears? I am not worried about him; I am concerned about the two females because one of them is a forensic pathologist. The troopers can look after themselves."

"In that I agree, DCS," the Commander said. "I will have everything covered from my end. We will be able to launch an emergency evacuation should the need arise."

"Have you had any result concerning the two bad guys who were keeping an eye on them?"

"Yes and no. We are sorting through the details. All we have managed to gain so far is the fact that a large mining company employs them as security advisers."

"I'm requesting that you keep them under lock and key as long as you can. I find it strange that these two have not as yet asked for a lawyer."

"Yes that is a question we must have answered sooner rather than later DCS."

"On that note, I'll get on with it Benson out."

Steve then sat down with Al Philips to discuss the progress so far. They kicked it around for the better part of an hour and a half before giving it up. "I'll have to let Jimmy have his head. He will not take kindly to too much interference from me or the system. Overall, I'm pleased we have made some progress. We had nothing to start with, and I believe we have come a long way forward. However, this could be wishful thinking," Steve said. "I'm going to talk to Jerry to find out how his end is holding up."

Using the two-way radio, Steve called Jerry back at the office. With the preliminaries over, Steve asked Jerry had he made any progress at all tracking Stains' itinerary.

"Yes boss," Jerry told Steve, "it appears in the past that Stains has lived in Yellowknife, Wrigley, and Fort Providence. His family line goes back almost to the beginning of Canada's history. His family still have business interests across the Northwest Territories."

Can you list these business interests? That might give it another angle to work. It might highlight any family feuds that are boiling under the surface. In any case, send me a list of his family activities there is a fax machine here to be if you can do it that way. It is not much more we can do at the moment, so I'll stand by and wait to receive it." It was two hours before the list came from Jerry.

In keeping with what Jerry had sent, Steve and Al used the the information to divide the local map into grid squares for the search. As soon as the maps were finished each searcher was given a copy and sent on their way, it was at least keeping them occupied. 20 minutes after that one of the searchers called base on the two-way radio.

Whatever the message is, I do not want it sent over an open channel. Just give me the grid square number and stand by there until you hear from me. Is that understood?"

"Yes boss, message understood, over and out."

CHAPTER 4

Back at RCMP HQ, Jerry Armstrong was going making an effort to get everything sorted with some help from the Tech dept to not only be ready to receive any transmissions from the boss and the team in the Northwest Territories, but have it sorted in the right file required. That is a reference file for the system, a file for the squad room and a legal file for the Attorney General's office to be used for the prosectution of anyone caught in the RCMP's net.

He was just starting to organize himself when he had a visit from the AC.

"Good morning DS Armstrong, how are things with you."

"Slow sir, but I'm getting there."

"Would you like some extra help?"

"That would be great but it must be somebody I can work with. I have a suggestion which may be out of order but I would like you to consider it. Perfect for me would be my wife from the Tech office, who is also trained IT expert."

"That's an excellent idea, I will go back an organiser now uncovered transferred to this area temporarily. You see you don't know what you'll get if you do not ask."

With that, the AEC was off leaving Jerry to continue. About half an hour later his wife came in the door with a smile, saying, "What do you know I've just been transferred to you on a temporary basis to help you set up the recording of the files and the legal documents when there required."

"That's fantastic. Now I have three laptops set up we need to have one ready as in a hostage up operation to record any phone calls or reports from the Northern Territory. The second laptop to be set up to the squad room here for the access for the members looking for information. The third one to be set up to contain the legal file for the Attorney General's office. I will cover the one for the squad room and one for the AG's office if you can hook up the third one to record any phone calls or reports coming in."

"That's easy Jerry, I'll get on with it now."

The rest of the morning was spent between the two of them getting the machines ready. Jerry thought that it was very pleasant working with my wife they were getting on with no problems which was even better. Half the rest of the day was used up getting everything sorted and tested and ready for use. Jerry gave his wife the earlier recording of reports and phone conversation with Steve Benson and after a sorted out put in the appropriate file. "I am going to call Steve Benson the boss in the Northwest Territories now to let him know that everything is set from this point forward. Base calling number one over," Jerry said on air using the radio. He had to repeat the message twice more before he had an answer.

Over the airwaves came the familiar voice, "Number one receiving over."

Jerry replied, "just to let you know boss everything is set for all your reports and phone calls to be recorded here into three separate files. One for the squad room, one a record any phone calls and reports, and one for the legal file for the Attorney General's office. A recording coming from your end will be recorded automatically so no information should be lost. By the way I have a helper courtesy of the AC from the technical department my wife would you believe?"

"Excellent Jerry, I have to go now because were under fire from some of the bad guys. I will talk to you again, Benson out"

Jerry picked up the phone and dialled the AC's office. When the AC came online Jerry said, "Armstrong sir, I have just been trying to talk to DCS Benson, he told me he didn't have time because he was under fire again."

"Yes," the AC said, "I know about that. The CC and I are putting together a plan to give him more help up there. Until we do I know he will make every effort to protect himself and his people, and to hell with the rules. So don't worry help is on the way."

"Apart from that I have three laptops set up to record everything that comes in the office. One to record phone calls and reports from Northwest Territories, one for the squad room, and once set up to create a prosecution file for the Attorney General's office. That means that every communication comes in this office will be recorded somewhere. So that at the end he will not waste any time putting together a legal case for the Attorney General. I would also like to thank you for transferring Mrs Armstrong to this squad for the time being. This is a sort of thing I should have done earlier, never mind it is done now."

"Excellent DS Armstrong, I will call in occasionally to see how you are getting on. On that note I will let you get on with it," the A/C said and broke the connection.

"Now as a test of the system was that call and the one a merely to the boss recorded as as they should have been?"

"Yes, Jerry, everything looks to be working fine."

CHAPTER 5

"Now that the map has been divided into grid squares, let's sit down and check grid square 14 on the map. That particular grid square is north-east one third the way out of Wrigley to Keller lake. It should only take about 30 minutes to get there. Saddle up we will head for there now." Over the air Steve said, "a general message to all units from No 1, I will be at grid square 14 if you are looking for me." Then Steve and Al left to catch up with whatever had been found at grid square 14."

Two trails lead off into the Bush from a corner of grid square 14. A trooper had his snowmobile hidden from view to conceal his presence when the two officers arrived. As the two officers approached his position, he stepped out from hiding to flag them down.

"Hold on boss, when I get my snowmobile. We have to go a little way into the Bush."

As soon as the trooper made an appearance, Steve and Al fell in behind. They went about a kilometre down one of the tracks before the trooper stopped, got off his machine and pointed to his right and took off on foot. After about 100 meters he stopped and pointed to the ground. The earth had been disturbed showing a partial skeleton, part of the ribcage and what looked like part of an arm.

Steve told the trooper to return to the fork in the trail and act as a guard, just in case.

Steve pointed the speaker/receiver of his radio clipped to his collar to his mouth. "General message from No1. Sergeant Stephens come and join us at grid square 14 ASAP." To Al, he said, "I am going to talk to Yellowknife to have them uplift Jimmy and the two ladies here to join us. We need the doc for the remains and Jimmy to have a good look at whatever tracks are left. I'm going to leave Jill at the base to be the contact with Jerry and to man the office, as the listening post."

"AI can you relieve the trooper guarding the way in, and send them here so I can have it talk to him."

Al was just about to leave when Sergeant Stephens arrived. "You made good time getting here. I want you to look at what has been found. Then I want you to relieve the trooper guarding the way and send him here. I want to question him on how he found the gravesite. Once I have a few answers, I will want you to remain here as guard. I will leave two more troopers because I want this burial site protected against all comers. Standing order of the day is, 'I want you to arrest anyone who comes within rifle'. I have all the information to be had, and Doctor Connors our pathologist has examined the area I will have the remains, and the rest of you moved back to the RCMP base. When DS Two Bears arrives, I want you to be his assistant. This light snowfall is a pain, and it may obliterate any sign on the ground but we have to try."

When the trooper arrived, Steve left it to AI to grill the RCMP B trooper for about 15 minutes on how or why he found the gravesite. Trooper Joe Bascal had found a leg bone and some animal tracks leading away into the Bush. Out of curiosity, Bascal, decided to follow them resulting in him finding the gravesite. What made it easier was the fact that the whole search area had been broken down by the use of grid squares. Right from the start, Steve had made it very clear that anyone referring to a particular area when they used the two-way radio, that the grid square number only was to be put over the airwaves, hopefully, this would keep the opposition confused.

Just to confuse things a bit more, Steve had broken down the search area into West and East. Starting at the top end of the search area the first Western grid square was designated No1, and the first eastern square No2. With the squares of approximately equal size to each other, they were numbered using every other number. That put grid square number 14 near the bottom of the East side.

When Steve had as much information he was likely to have, he told Al that he was heading back to base to talk to Yellowknife. "Al, you hold on here till you hear from me. Maybe you could build a temporary roof over the gravesite to keep off as much snow as possible. That will leave three at the gravesite for security." Steve then left to return to the base camp at Wrigley, satisfied that everything was progressing.

It was a hard ride back to base, due to the waiting forming small snowdrifts, but Steve still made it with time to spare. Once inside the small barracks, Steve didn't stop to take off his outer storm gear. He picked up the radio Mike and put out the call sign for the RCMP base at Yellowknife. When the operator answered his call Steve identified himself and told the man at the other end to put it through to the Commandant immediately.

With the Commandant on air, Steve didn't waste any time." Benson here Sir. We have found another gravesite here in the area where the person we are looking for went missing. I need my pathologist Doctor Conners, and Jimmy Two Bears here now. Can you have my three individuals and their equipment uplifted by air to Wrigley immediately? It is snowing in the area where the grave site is located, so the sooner I can have the team here the better."

Understood DCS. I have access to a chopper that can deliver them in a couple of hours or less."

So nothing went over the air, Steve said, "these are either the remains of the person we are looking for, or another unsolved murder that has escaped detection," Steve told him.

"I'll let you get on with it so I can organise the uplift of your team. Talk to you soon, DCS. Yellowknife out."

Steve then called Al Philips to find out how things were progressing. Al reported that the light snowstorm had stopped, but he had formed a branch roof over the site anyway.

"Great Al. When the rest of the team arrive, they can leave the bulk of their equipment here. Hopefully, the bad guys have not as yet caught on to what we are doing. Nevertheless, keep the perimeter guarded. Make sure you and the others have a hot drink or soup. I'm going to get the trooper patrolling the end of the grid square 14, to report to base to act as backup for Jill who I am going to leave at the base in Wrigley, but there must be somebody closer that I can use."

Steve made super himself while he waited for the team to arrive the chopper came out of the mist and landed in an open space about 100 meters from the building. He had the equipment and ordered quickly with all hads chipping in. The chopper was on its way again with the loss of only 30 minutes. Steve had coffee brewing, so he let them catch their breath while he brought them up to date.

"How did you find the site, even if the snow was light, it would surely obliterate any sign?" Jimmy wanted to know.

"An old Eagle eye like yourself. We have several troopers on loan. One of whom Joe Bascal found a leg bone it in his grid square and tracks leading back into the Bush. He marked the spot we found the bone before he followed the animal tracks back to the gravesite."

"So helpfully, Donna can give us an ID using DNA. Also, Al reports that it has stopped snowing. But to make sure I had Al build a temporary roof over the site, which has been overlaid by a thin layer of snow, making it look like the surrounding Bush. Donna, now we have the other snowmobiles, we will take all your forensic equipment whether we use whether or not we use it."

"Jill I want you to man the base here. Order of the day contact Jerry back at HQ and ask to set up a direct link between himself and you here, using a laptop computer so that information is logged directly into our system. We are going to lose some of the information that we don't start getting it into our system now. I need you to do this Jill as you are apart from Jerry, are our most competent computer operator."

"I agree boss I will contribute more here than I would do it."

Steve then called Al, to let him know they were heading back to the gravesite, and to also have him send trooper Armstrong and snowmobile back to Wrigley base as a backup for Jill. Steve got on air again, "I want one more trooper who is close to base to report directly to base ASAP." When Armstrong arrived, there would be three RCMP at the base, Troopers Armstrong, 1 more trooper and Jill. With the two highly experienced troopers, they should be able to defend themselves. He thought as soon as I have one more trooper free I will send him to the base to bolster the numbers.

Steve told them he would give Armstrong 15 minutes to arrive at the base before they left. He had not want to leave Jill in a position where she couldn't defend herself. As soon as the trooper arrived, Steve gave them instructions about setting up a perimeter with the base now more secure he told the rest to head out for grid square 14. Steve was happier now that experienced troopers were guarding the station making Jill's position safer. She was a female officer of the RCMP and should be competent enough to protect herself, but that still does not mean she should be left without help. Now with extra RCMP troopers, she would be able to concentrate on being logged into their system and also to act as their radio listening post.

CHAPTER 6

The small group from Wrigley (Steve, Jimmy, and Donna) on the way back to the gravesite had only gone about 800 meters when several shots kicked up snow around the small convoy. The sound of their snowmobiles and the snow covered any noise the rifles would have made when fired. Without hesitation, as the rounds seemed to have come from his right Steve pointed with his left had and moved that way deeper into the Bush. He wanted to stay within rifle range of the shooter or shooters. While Jimmy quickly formed a perimeter guard, Steve called Jill to make sure the base was still functioning. Just in case. Steve was confident their heavy weather outer clothing would camouflage them and make them difficult targets to hit.

The snowmobile engines shut down, an uneasy calm settled over the small group. Two more rounds kicked up snow to their right side front. Jimmy, as usual, was waiting and fired two shots at their point of origin to be rewarded when they heard one of the opposition shout as if he might have been hit, followed by the sound of two snowmobiles starting up their engines. Jimmy fired four more rounds in that direction just to make sure the opposition were vacating the area. Also all sounds quickly died as the snow machines moved away.

Steve called the base to check on them. It was one of the troopers who answered the call. Without wasting time or words, Steve told the RCMP trooper that they had come under attack, and to Batten down the hatches. "Pass the word to Jill to leave the computer work for now just Batten down the hatches so you can defend yourselves in case you come under attack." Steve then put out a general call to have another trooper join Jill just in case.

"No1 to all troopers, stop what you are doing and report to grid square 14. I want the one nearest the Wrigley barracks to report there I don't want to waste time now, explanations will come later."

Trooper Jim Henry on air said, "I can head over there now. I can be there in 10 minutes boss."

"Do that," was all Steve said.

Before moving out, Steve made sure Donna was wearing her bulletproof vest. T. Hen throwing caution to the wind he made the gesture with his arm to go to the gravesite as quickly as possible.

There was no sign of anybody at the gravesite until Al Philips poked his head up from under the snow. As there were only three of them, Al and the Sergeant and one trooper, they could have been in serious trouble if they had come under attack. So, the best thing they could have done was to make themselves into snow bunnies.

Steve told the Sergeant to set up a perimeter guard, as soon as he made the introductions. The Sergeant through being part of the survival course run by Jimmy was pleased that they had Jimmy Two Bears on our side. Steve noted that there was a certain amount of rapport between the two. Steve then took the time to find out how the Wrigley base camp was doing.

Report was that everything was quiet now. Steve warned them that they could not afford to relax, that the absence of sound might be the calm before the storm. "Jill you have three experienced officers there make use of them, but none the less ensure you are set up to repel all borders to protect yourselves at all costs. No1 is listening out."

Steve left Donna to examine the gravesite. Later she told Steve, "This person was male according to the bone structure, about 5'10" that corresponds to the description I have of Stains. You brought the files with you so I should be able to do a rough crosscheck here. It may turn out to be inaccurate, but our current position is not ideal. Give me at least 15 to 30 minutes, and I should be able to make a comparison."

"Al put out a perimeter guard; I will stay here to cover Donna."

Donna was almost finished doing a DHA profile on the body remains when two shots were fired at her position. Steve had made sure that she would not be in a position where she come under a direct attack. As Steve was off to one side, he picked up the approximate position of the shooter or shooters. He fired six rounds rapidly to that area. One of the others did the same, and they were rewarded by the sound of what could only have been a death cry.

On air, Steve said, "This is No1, I will hold my position. The rest of you using caution move out to where you think the shooters were hiding."

Al and Jimmy moved out first leaving the others to watch their backs. Jimmy was first find the person left behind. He was dead from having being hit at least twice in his chest area. Jimmy reported the fact to Steve over the radio.

Donna had removed the rest of the snow covering the remains so she could get to work. When the team had extracted as much information as could be had from the area, Steve ordered them to pack up ready to head back to base. Under Donna's direction, the body remains were carefully picked up and placed in one of the trailer and covered by a small tarp; then Donna was ready to go. Steve gave the order to move out. He had Al lead, and Jimmy bring up the rear with himself in the middle. They wasted no time returning to base.

With the three troopers that Steve had sent to cover the base, and with himself, Al, Jimmt, Jill, the sergeant and two more constables, there ws a strength of ten to protect the outpost. Steve had the sergeant draw up a schedule for a perimeter guard. Once done Steve could now relax and focus on trying to find out whose remains they had found.

CHAPTER 7

It was in 2012 the year he died, politician Gregory Stains arrived in Wrigley on the second half of his official visit on behalf of the Minister for First Nations Affairs. There had been several incidents involving members of first nations and prospectors over land claims due to the finding of rare minerals particularly diamonds and gold in small deposits, on land that was the sole property of the local First Nations.

Stains had an unemployment the first day with Tom Reynolds who was the order of a small supply business and a licensed assay office. Although Reynolds and several prominent citizens waited a couple of hours for Stains, he was a no-show. It was several hours before Reynolds reported the absence of St to authorities. Unfortunately, some time was lost before an official search was put in place.

In spite of calling in volunteers, additional RCMP officers, and the State Rescue Service no trace of Stains was found. Due to the fact of Stains official status in the government, the current Governor of N WT kept the search going for a month, with no result. Soon after the search was terminated, the file was marked open/unsolved and sent to the RCMP HQ with a copy to the Government Archives.

The group that waited that fateful day for Stains, had a list of complaints about the inefficiencies of the State Treasury, as regards the quality of gold ore and rough diamonds. Wales could get around the gold by doing any number of tests of the metal, but the diamonds were another thing. The diamonds had to be transported to the capital to be assayed by diamond merchants, and several shipments had gone missing. Reynolds could no longer afford the payments for insurance coverage. That was why he and the other business owners needed to have an in-depth talk to Stains, to voice their displeasure with how the Government was hadling the whole process.

Stains was picked up from his guesthouse the morning of his death and a local business owner who was to take him to the meeting with Reynolds. Stains found two other men were waiting in the limo when Stains got in. The driver took them to a spot North of Wrigley, where they wanted stains to inspect a prospecting claim which the First Nations could prove was on their land. The area was a 3 km² piece of scrubland north-east of Wrigley, close to Keller Lake. Stains had to walk the last half kilometre to get there. When the small group was sufficiently off the beaten track, one of the men hit Stains on the back of the head with a piece of iron bar. Stains was dead before he hit the ground. The killers made sure he was dead before picking up his body and throwing it into a hollow in the ground. Then they covered him with loose soil. Satisfied there would be a long time before, or if, anyone from found the remains.

The men made sure they left no physical evidence of their presence before heading back to Wrigley to go their separate ways. This group agreed once they went their different ways they would never meet, so the trail as far as th RCMP investigation was concerned went cold, at that point.

A crime syndicate who were striving to control all the gold and diamonds unearthed in the Northwest Territories had instigated this whole scenario. The may have gotten away with their crime except to the fact that Sta was a member of the Legislative Council. From that standpoint, his death would not go unnoticed. There was also the considerable pressure brought to bear by the Stains family. Senior police knew that because of his status in the community they would not be allowed to treat his death and disappearance as a casual event. As a cold case, it would stay on the books, for as long or until it was brought to a satisfactory conclusion.

Some of the more level headed members of the crime syndicate wanted stains roughed up and given his marching orders out of the N WT but the hot heads had had their way. Therefore, Stains life was terminated. This action was not going to let them off the hook as they soon found once Steve Benson was on their trail. When that happened they would find out quickly enough that Benson and his team did not give up easily.

Due to the timelapse between when Stains died and the present, a lot of time had been lost, so the trail was long cold when Benson eventually became involved in the investigation. Steve was going to have a look at every aspect of Stains' life no matter how minute to try and draw a lie across that life that had been Gregory Stains life no matter how minute to try and draw a line across that life that had been Gregory Stains. The primary complaint of Stains constituents was the fact the quality of gold when assayed was not the same gold as was offered for sale later. Stains knew that the only way to prove this was to try to follow a small amount of gold from the mine to the product in the jeweller's shop, or Government bank vault storage. Unfortunately, this could not be said of the diamonds. Discoveries of gold and diamonds was a magnet for the criminal underworld.

At Wrigley base, it was easier for Donna to give a more accurate conclusion to a DNA report on the skeletal remains. "I am very confident that this was Stains," Donna told Steve, "But does that help you at all knowing that fact?"

Picking up the phone, Steve dialled the number of his office. On the third ring of familiar voice said, "Cold Case Squad, DS Armstrong speaking."

"This is the boss here. Start the recorder for this. Steve waited to be told he was being recorded before giving an in-depth report on events to date. When he finished, he told Jerry to have a look at every aspect of the history of Gregory Stains. "There has to be a connection which leads up to the present. Ignore everything else, this has total priority."

Just then, Jerry interrupted Steve to tell him the AC had just walked in. "Good Jerry put on the line please."

Steve said, "Benson Sir, this will save me the trouble of another phone call." Steve then described the attacks on the group by persons unknown. Result two bad guys downed and no casualties on our side."

"That is a relieve DCS. But where does that leave us?"

"Up the proverbial Creek. What I need from you is for me to have total access to be able to rummage around in government archives to try to find an answer as to why somebody is still interested in what happened to Stains after all this time."

"I agree Steve. I will talk to the Commissioner now and let you know what success ASAP. AC out." The commission returned the handpiece to Jerry and left the office.

With Jerry back on the line Steve asked had his conversation with the A/C being recorded.

"Yes Sir. I have set up the machinery the way we would if this was a hostage situation where every incoming or outgoing call is recorded automatically. So no information should be lost. The A/C was good enough to lend me an extra per of hads to set it all up, who just happens to be my wife. Isn't that good?"

"That's good Jerry, we will get permission to be able to dig into all government archives without interference from political bosses. So keep on trying to find out as much as you can about Stains' past. If you have any problems I will try to get as much pressure to bear as possible from the CC where I can. When you have done that, try and do the same for the young couple Sean and Sally Adams whose remains were discovered South of Aylmer Lake North of Reliance in the N WT. I believe you'll find that there is a relationship between the two parties."

CHAPTER 8

Steve sat in the Wrigley RCMP Post waiting to hear from Donna. He had already told her to take her time as they had plenty now. It was the second day, of relative calm when rifle fire could be heard from outside the building.

"That came from the direction of one of the guard positions." AI pointed out. On air I'll said, "This is No2 have we come to their studies under attack of any kind, all guards report their status."

All guard positions indicated clear, accept for the one manned by Joe Bascal. He reported that he had discovered he was under the watch by an unlown the so he fired in that direction and was rewarded by the sound of a snowmobile moving away. To protect himself as soon as he shot at the opposition, he changed his position so they couldn't do a Jimmy and return fire to his location. All he could report was that he found no trace of the opposition when he got to the approximate position of the other person.

"Jimmy, you and the Sergeant and Jim Henry, go out quietly and do a recce. One left, and one right with you in the middle Jimmy. Get your heads together and decide how you want to cover the area. If you happen to find anyone, arrest them and drag them back here. Off you go." Steve ordered.

Jimmy and his two companions moved out like shadows. It was the Sergeant who found a bunch of three men that looked to be laying up in ambush. It seemed as if they were waiting for Steve and his men to come searching for them. The Sergeant gave the bird whistle agreed on as meaning come to my position. He kept bird whistling until the other two made their way there next to him. When they were next to the Sergeant and back in their allotted position, Jimmy quietly gave the order of the day being "They were to try and bring them back alive if possible."

Jimmy fired two shots over the heads of the attack and in a voice that from the other side of the grave said out loud, "Surrender now or be sent to hell. You are under attack by a superior force. Show yourselves if you wish to live."

The Sergeant said quietly, "That was well done Jimmy." Then the first head popped up from under the snow, followed by the whole bunch who was now exposed and stood with their hads in the air.

Using a small canvas sack, Jimmy then ordered the attackers to put the rest of their weapons into the bag and to lay down their long guns in the snow. Or, nine attackers altogether, six under the snow and the three that were already under arrest. One of the men whispered, we could have taken them," before Jimmy gave him a blow to the back of his head." That was for thinking that we were a bunch of amateurs." While he had them on the ground, Jimmy cable tied hads and feet; now they were not about to go anywhere.

"I'm going to call the boss to bring him up to date. First order of the day, if they try to move shoot them. If they ignore you shoot to kill." For good measure, Jimmy fired several shots in the air. Jimmy walked further away keeping the group in sight regardless. When he had Steve on the air, he quickly explained the situation.

"Can you hold till help gets there?"

"Yes boss."

"Stand fast, No1 out."

Steve called the others to take a couple of snowmobiles and trailers to carry the prisoners back to base. At the base camp, one of Steve's men had erected a tent with no sides. The attackers were dumped around the central tent pole where everyone could keep an eye on them.

Steve got on the radio to Yellowknife to talk to the Commandant. When he got an answer, Steve said, "Good morning Sir, I have captured another nine attackers. I need them uplifted by air to your position for interrogation and charging. We are in a bind at the moment, as we have no place to hold them securly, so ASAP if possible."

"Understood, rescue is on the way." Yellowknife out.

"Jimmy fire a couple of rounds every now and then over their heads to keep them in line," Steve told Jimmy. Fortunately, the chopper was there within 30 minutes. It arrived just as more bad guys decided to attack the base hut.

Steve picked up the radio, "Base one to chopper, stand-off I repeat stand-off. We are under attack. Report situation to Yellowknife assistance required ASAP. No1 out"

The chopper, which was not armed, showing good judgement; stood off just out of rifle rage, just as the radio spoke. "Commander, Yellowknife, report your situation and casualty numbers."

"Benson here Sir. Have no idea of the strength of the opposition we are pinned down in the base building. I ordered our chopper to stand-off till I hear from you Benson standing by out"

The commander in Yellowknife put out an urgent call for the Chief Commissioner. Once he had him on air, he quickly put gave a report and put a demand in for more help from the military. The CC told him to stand fast while he started organising heavy weapons. "Directly attacking our system of law and order has got to stop before every lowlife in Canada thinks he can declare war on the

RCMP." He made that point forcibly when he spoke directly to the General Commanding the multipurpose gunship units. The general then spoke directly with Commander Paxton in Yellowknife, at the same time he was instructing his Flag Officer which group to launch. By the end of the phone call, four Blackhawk choppers had already been deployed. They arrived in short order and did an aerial recon to assess situation.

It was just as well as Steve's group had sustained minor casualties and were going getting low on ammo.

Captain Dixon, the aerial commander, called Wrigley base. "Air one calling ground one over."

"Ground one receiving over."

"The heaviest concentration is your left flank. We will keep that flank occupied; you concentrate on your right flank. Air one over and out."

Steve credited in the middle of the room and got everyone's attention. "I want at least two volunteers to take the fight up to the opposition. The idea is to exit the building quietly and do try to find the opposition." All three Jack Armstrong, Jim Henry, and Joe Bascal where the first to fifth put up there hads. To Al Philips, Steve said, "You hold the Fort while Jimmy, Jack, Joe and I sneak out to take up the fight. AI for some ribbon or tape to use as armbands, then the rest of you should be able to recognise us in the field. All set up with different armbands Steve gave them the last plan of attack, before going out a rear window that was shielded from view by a rock overhang. They moved in a wide arc before moving in towards the attacker's positions. They took out four of the opposition before the opposition realised they were on rear.

An attempt to protect themselves when they moved the armbands allowed Steve and his men and the shooters in the base at to take the Majority of the opposition down either dead or wounded. The two remaining lifted their arms in surrender after putting their weapons on the ground. Steve made sure they are all of their mouths taped so they could not shout out a warning to the rest. He was not worried about the dead, and the living would be seen to when they had this situation under control.

"Ground one to air one, are you receiving this?" Steve said into his microphone.

"Air one receiving over."

Ground one, we have the situation under control on the left flank. Take the rest down now. Let us conclude this. Ground No1 out."

"Message received and understood, air No1 out."

The choppers proceeded to attack with greater vigor. In no time due to the opposition, sustaining heavy casualties they grounded their weapons and surrendered. Steve called the senior military officer to send in the two picked up the bodies, while the walking wounded were frogmarched out of the area where they would be picked up and taken to a detention centre already set up for the purpose.

With everything underway, Steve called his boss the AC. Steve first said hello and then gave a copy of the report of what had happened.

"Stand firm Steve while I speak to the CC." Steve waited another 10 minutes before the familiar voice of the CC came online.

"Been getting into mischief again, DCS. But yo the sustained no serious injuries, that's a good outcome. Calling in the military was a very with while the. But still at this point we have no idea who is behind this?"

"No Sir. We may do when some of them have been interrogated. This is not a guaranteed fact. We may in fact have to resort to executing some violence on their person, as a way to get them to open up."

"I didn't hear that," the CC told Steve. "One thing I am going to do is to send you more we enforcement, with all necessary equipment for an extended stay in the wilderness. I have already put this in motion, so the first of them should arrive early tomorrow. Our political bosses thankfully are on the same page as us. You will in fact, have a force of almost 200 both RCMP and Rangers under your command. As the senior ranking officer, the word has been passed out that they were to obey all you can field, no exceptions."

As soon as he put down the phone, Steve had Al and Jimmy Two Bears join him in the small office that was part of the main building. Once inside and the door closed, Steve explained about the additional troops that were to join them. "AI you are now the official 2IC and Jimmy will be recognised as the senior Sergeant. As soon as the Army arrives, I will have them in here for a briefing. Al get hold of the current body in charge of the military that are here now and wheel him in."

As soon as AI returned with a Lieutenant Major from the Ranger Corp who introduced himself as L.T. George Bowes.

Lt Bowes I want you under the eye of Al Philips to use your men are still corrected tented camp for the additional incoming troops that are on their way. They will also bring extra equipment whether we use it or not. Draw up a guard roster to act as snow bunnies in the heavy winter clothing we already have. I want them to disappear into the scenery; I am sure I do not have to spell it out for you. "Al get hold of Jimmy Two Bears, who is a First Nation's Tribal Chief, looking at Bowes, "and introduce him to our friend here."

LT Bowes I want you to be directed by whatever Jimmy suggests because he is a wilderness survival expert. Off you go and get started; I'll wait for the rest of the additional incoming troops to arrive."

Satisfied for the moment, Steve sat down to write a report for the AC and the CC. He had hardly started before the sound of incoming choppers brought him to his feet again. He went outside to join Al and LT Bowes ready to greet the incoming troops. When all the troopers and equipment was unloaded, an army Major came up to were Steve and co were standing and said, "I'm looking for a Detective Chief Superintendent Benson."

"I'm Benson, Major," Steve said.

The Major gave a smart salute and said, "I'm Major Brian Fawkner Canadian Ranger Corp reporting as ordered, Sir"

Steve acknowledged with a return salute and shook the Major's had. "This is my two IC Detective Inspector Alan Philips. As the two men shook hads Steve said to AI; "I'm taking the Major inside for an in-depth talk, keep everybody outside and working." Steve followed with; "There is one other person on my staff I would like to introduce Detective Sergeant Jimmy Two Bears, a first nations tribal chief, and a wilderness survival expert."

The Major said, "Hello Jimmy," as he shook Jimmy's had. The Sergeant and I are old friends due to attending Jimmy's survival course twice."

Now with the formalities or the two senior ranks went inside the small RCMP barracks. "Let's get rid of the formalities; you can call me boss or Steve whichever is easier."

"I will answer to Brian when we are long and Major when we are in front of the troops. A little bird tells me that you are pretty good at tracking bad people in the frozen North, and you are a retired former Marine."

"Yes to both accounts," Steve told him.

Steve got up and fetched 2 cups of coffee for them before sitting down and giving the Major an in-depth report on the current situation. Steve told Fawkner there was no need to take notes, as he would give a copy of the report he was sending to the Canadian CC of the RCMP and the police service.

The two men kicked the problem around for the better part of an hour before a consensual agreement was reached about what would be the order of business and the flow of information, and importantly the chain of command. Steve already had an extended map of the area spread out on the table. Because Steve was addressing a military commander, he did not have to worry about map coordinates and compass bearings.

"When we first got attacked it was from this quarter. Using Jimmy Two Bears' superior tracking skills, I would like you to swing out in a full arc dividend cut across the direction the attackers took, either coming or going. With a bit of luck, we could track them to their lair before we bring in the heavy equipment. It is up to you, but if you could pick a team of 10 men with hard experience in the frozen North adequately equipped for winter warfare, we could maybe shorten this engagement."

"Excellent idea, Steve. I'll go now and get it underway."

"I'll come with you and have a word with Jimmy before you go. Don't worry if Jimmy goes out ahead and you think you may have lost him; don't worry about looking for him, he will find you. You can work out the details between you. All and one thing, he doesn't like formality just call him Jimmy. So let's get this show on the road," Steve said as he led the way outside.

Steve left the Major to talk to his troops while he had a word with his team. The campsite was already underway to being finished. Steve and the Major had agreed that everyone understood the first rule that they look for the point of origin instead of worrying about being under fire. Steve explained that it was Jimmy that had added this twist successfully.

CHAPTER 9

With the camp strategically guarded by concealed submachine guns mounted on 360° tripods, everything was set with a siege in mind. With everyone settled in, the campsite was quiet for two days until the evening of the second day, when they came under direct attack from the East quarter at around 7.30pm in the evening. It was not so much that the bad guys doing the shooting, as the return fire from the submachine guns that grabbed everyone's attention.

In no time, the firing from the opposition became less against the sound of departing snowmobiles. The military had already split to form a pincer movement and was warming in for a more direct attack. With one last push, they walked into where the enemy position had been. They found several dead and wounded. The wounded were quickly rounded up searched for IDs as well as being frisked for hidden weapons they may have been carrying and made to sit in a group.

Donna as the resident Doctor checked all the dead to make sure there were no signs of life. The military had brought body bags as a precaution, so the Major selected a small group onerous to put the bodies into the body bag and then lined them up along the sidewall of the RCMP barracks. Due to the low temperature leaving them outside was equal to putting the remains into a refrigerator.

While Donna patched up the wounded on both sides, Steve contacted the A/C about picking up both the bodies and the injured to clear the site. The opposition would be taken away for interrogation before being charged and sent to prison.

In the middle of all this, Steve had Jimmy go out a couple of kilometres accompanied by Stephens the other RCMP Sergeant to see if he could track the bad guys. They were back in three hours to report that as long as it didn't snow, they could maybe have some success. It appeared that the opposition had taken off in a Northeasterly direction. So with a bit of caution to follow behind them, to their lair. "If you could spring the use of a chopper, I would like Sergeant Stephens and me to go out at first way to do a recce from the air," Jimmy told Steve.

The Major who was sitting in during Jimmy's debriefing said, "I'll go and organise the chopper now DCS, and bring the pilot back for any more instructions you want to give." The Major went off to get hold of the best chopper pilot who was part of the group. After a short talk, they went back to the barracks to report to Steve.

Steve addressing the chopper pilot made sure that once in the air the pilot was to follow any instructions given by Jimmy as long as the safety of the aircraft was not compromised. Around dawn, the following morning the chopper took off with machine gunners riding shotgun on both sides of the helicopter. It followed the path that Jimmy would have taken on foot in a northeasterly direction. Jimmy asked the pilot to fly higher and slower so he could more easily read the sign in the snow.

They had covered about 15 km when Jimmy asked the pilot to swing around in a full arc. He had the pilot fly the same arc three times before hover over a particular spot. Into his microphone, he said, "Have a look down now, you can see where the group of bad guys has separated into two halves before going in different directions."

Jimmy tossed a coin for heads or tails and asked the pilot to pick. The pilot chose heads, which turned up. "Okay pick the group you want to follow, but mark this spot on your map. We will probably have to fly over the other track at some time."

The pilot chose the right-had group and continued to fly after them under Jimmy's direction. After another 5 or 6 km, Jimmy lost the sign. To the pilot, he said, "Put down somewhere convenient, the Sergeant and I will track them on foot for a time the see if we can pick up the trial."

The chopper put down onto the snow very gently so as not to disturb any sign on the ground. Jimmy and the Sergeant were dressed in Arctic survival clothing, and as both were seasoned winter experts, they couldn't or shouldn't get into any trouble. Besides, they could always call the chopper for a pickup. They separated with about 50 meters between them and did a slow march alongside what was an indistinct trail. They carried on for about 5 km before Jimmy called a halt. The chopper had taken off and was shadowing them just out of rifle range. Jimmy put his arm up and pointed in the general direction he thought the bad guys had taken and said into his radio, "Air one go in this general direction, for about 15 kms to looksee and report. We will follow on foot. Then you can come back and pick us up."

There didn't seem to be any doubt which direction the opposition was headed. It looked like the attackers were heading to Norman Wells or Fort Good Hope, before possibly crossing the county border into Nunavat. Jimmy called the chopper back for a pickup.

Once on the ground, Jimmy had the pilot climb down so he could discuss what they were going to do next. With the map spread out on the floor of the chopper Jimmy told the pilot that he believed the bad guys were headed in the direction of Norman Wells or Fort Good Hope.

"This is up to you," Jimmy said. Do you have enough fuel for us to do a recce to both places? If you have, we could have a looksee. But we would need to swing out in a wide arc, so the opposition doesn't know we are on to them. We may find the mining camp they are using as a base. You have cameras on board so we could get some aerial photos to take back. Then I would like you to backtrack along the same route back to Wrigley. I would like to take them by surprise if possible."

"I have enough fuel for this will exercise, so we can be off as soon as you are ready. Jimmy, you can stand up between the co-pilot and me so you can see from the front. You may pick up something we missed." The pilot told him. With everything set, they were off. Back at base Jimmy was able to tell Steve, what they had been doing and to show off the photographs as well, when they were developed. It would give Steve a more accurate picture of what he needed to do for the next phase. It would also give Steve more proof to put in the report to the A/C next time he made one. This would hopefully give Steve a good starting point from which to move forward. Not for the first time Jimmy thought I am glad it is not my decidion to make.

CHAPTER 10

Sean Louis Moreau, a distinguished looking man of 58 years, was standing enjoying the view from his 12 floor. He looked the epitome of a Chairman of the Board and who was also the Managing Director of his Company. His uncle Henry, mother's older brother, had bequeathed to best business to SL Moreau this current CEO. The company HQ offices were spread over two floors, with a broad connecting staircase between the two levels of this high rise office building in the central business district of Montréal City. Unfortunately, the current moral did not have a flair for running a mining and construction business like his uncle, and was inclined to cut corners that sometimes were outside the legal limits for conducting a business enterprise.

While he reminisced, there was a knock on the hit the office door before his secretary with a fax note in her had.

"Excuse me sir, this has just come in marked 'your eyes only,' his attractive middle-aged private secretary told him, as she passed across the sheet of paper. She waited in silence in case she was required.

Moreau read the paper several times before turning to the woman, "Grace find Joe Thompson and get him here ASAP."

His secretary left to get on with the task of finding Joe Thompson. Thompson was chief troubleshooter for Moreau. Whenever there was a problem concerning a work dispute or to settle a labour dispute,

Thompson would go in every time to resolve matters. It took the better part of 40 minutes to find Thompson. Grace got Thompson on the line she told him, "He requires your presence here urgently, Joe."

"Tell him I can be there in about an hour and a half." No goodbyes Joe just hung up the phone.

Grace got up from her desk, and after knocking on the door she went into Moreau's office and waited till boss looked up from his desk before she said, "Joe said he be here in an hour and a half."

"Thank you Grace, please ensure I am not disturbed until I call you."

"Yes Sir," Grace said and left quietly to return to her desk where from a drawer she pulled out a sign reading do not disturbed and had it on her boss's office door. When Thompson arrived, she mentioned for him to go straight in. Every time Grace saw Joe Thompson, regardless of what he was wearing, either work clothes or a suit he had that Canadian look of an outdoorsman. Grace not for the first time thought I would not like to run foul of Joe Thompson. Thompson tapped lightly on the door and went and went straight in.

Moreau haded over the fax sheet for Thompson to read and let him have a few minutes digesting the contents. When Thompson looked up his boss said, "I believed you had this under control?"

"I did boss. I have no idea what has gone wrong. I need to go up there and find out for myself why we have a problem."

Cancel everything else you are into, take the chopper and go find out." Moreau then pushed the switch for the intercom. When Grace answered he said, "Grace, fifth find the chopper pilot John Grayson, have come to see me urgently. Also tell them to make sure the chopper is in good flying order, as he will most likely be flying up into to the snow country."

The chopper in question was a modern all-weather executive machine, with a fully enclosed passenger cabin. Thompson also had a chopper license so between the two that they should be able to get themselves out of any trouble they may encounter. When the pilot arrived, Grace told him to go straight in.

After the usual pleasantries Moreau said, you will be flying to the edge of the Arctic Circle. The first thing I want you to do is to assemble the winter survival gear and get it installed aboard the chopper. You may have to camp out, so make sure you are carrying tents and sleeping bags. You know what is needed; off you go now and report when you are ready to leave."

The pilot left to get on with loading the chopper and getting the fifth ready to take off. He had done this in the past, so he was well aware of what was required. Some time would be lost travelling to the airport and packing the chopper, but then he could fly back to the heliport on the top of the building.

The helicopter was one of the latest Sikorsky S- 92 all-weather VIP aircraft, generally used by mining companies when prospecting for oil and gas deposits or to fly relief crews to and from oil rigs in the ocean.

Soon as the pilot left, Joe said, "I hadpicked that crew; there was enough of them to get the job done. I have no idea what went wrong. Anyway, there is no point speculating until I get it from the horse's mouth.

"Until you find out I am going to suspend work on the mine. Something I am reluctant to do, "his boss told him.

They sat there mulling over the current situation until security called to say the chopper had landed on the heliport on the roof of the building. "I'll be off, all I need is a day to find out what the problem is and report." With that, Thompson was gone.

After a quick discussion with the pilot, the chopper lifted off. Thompson directed the pilot to come in from the North of the last reported site where his men would be. When they reached that point, the pilot flew out in a full circle to check the area before coming into land. The problem was that there was no one left on the ground.

At the same time, Steve Benson had been busy rounding up 15 of the attackers and having them shipped back to the RCMP barracks in Wrigley to be guarded by the Canadian Rangers. They would be held there until arrangements could be made to send them back to the RCMP HQ to be questioned and charged before being indicted under whatever law covered their recent activities.

On the other had, Moreau in spite of a lack of business enterprise had taken the company passed the point where it was when he was haded the reins.

The small mine was Moreau's first venture into expanding the company he had started with a loan from the Moreau Family Trust. He had survived by cutting corners, aided and abetted by Thompson, altough on the surface he appeared to prosper. That was true of the mine. It was on land under the control of First Nations. That was why Thompson, Moreau's roustabout, had initially recruited 85 men who were miners from the oil and mining industries. The miners built two log cabins for accommodation disguised enough to make them appear to be part of the landscape. Some of the men were hunters and trappers so that they would could supply themselves with fresh meat and fish in abundance.

The best thing was that where no local settlements in the vicinity, so their activities went unnoticed. All the heavy machinery required was brought in by chopper in its component parts and assembled on site. The area was mostly wilderness, so getting rid of any spoil from the mine was not difficult. Thompson made sure that the miners were well paid, as his way of keeping them under control.

The mine was starting to yield some reasonable quantities of gold, all the more reason to keep its existence under wraps. It was the first time in life that Moreau had taken up a position in the slow Lane because even he realised the enormous potential of the mine. Steve Benson representing the law of Canada would eventually bring Moreau to the judge to be sentenced for his crimes.

One of the lean periods, he worked for the uncle would eventually bequeath the vast Moreau Construction Company to Séan Moreau. Once he got to that point, there was no stopping him. Also by then Moreau had set up a small criminal syndicate to further his control of local criminal gangs. This would give him more control for the illegal buying and selling of precious metals and oil. Initially all profits were ploughed back into payments for gang members until the whole business became profitable, he had achieved that now.

Moreau had used Stains and his political influence, to cut corners when it came to anything remotely connected to First Nations. It was especially true of any change in whichever way the political wind was blowing. However, once Stains and Reynolds the assayer realized that there could be diamonds involved their greed scale went up considerably.

It was this whole sorry list of events culminating in the death of Gregory and the Adams, which brought DCS Steve Benson into the equation. He would make sure justice was served. Unfortunately, events had been accelerated when Stains confronted Moreau, believing he could put down Moreau and take over his not so little criminal empire.

As it happened, it did not take Moreau long to have total control of the smaller Stains' family mine. He used a manager John Shepherd for the day-to-day activities who was by Thompson, and approved by his boss Moreau. Between them, they made a very capable trio of criminals. All Moreau had to do was to visit the mine as often as he could to make sure Stephens understood that he was the boss and he would brook no interference from anyone. Therefore, for the time being life was easy. Until that point, when Gregory Stains informed him that he had enough evidence to prove that Moreau was stealing form the mine assets.

Then Moreau wasted no time calling in Thompson and Shepherd for a Tete-a-tete to draw up a plan to permanently remove Gregory, Reynolds, the RCMP and anyone else who showed interest in his activities. However, this would not be enough to stop Steve Benson, just slow him down. In time, Jerry Armstrong would also find the link between Stains and Moreau, and more importantly between Gregory and the Adams.

Moreau's stupidity was the fact that he did not think that eliminating members of the RCMP, would be his undoing. There were enough detectives in RCMP to take up the challenge even if Steve Benson was taken out of the equation.

Steve called in Al, Jimmy, and the Major to his office to draw up the battle plan for the next step.

"As usual after giving more thought to this situation. I have decided to attach my sergeant and two extra Mounties to be the RCMP representatives who will keep everything legal from a police point of view. Let our people worry about that side. The sergeant will be given strict instructions not to do anything stupid without having the go-ahead from me. Will that do? The most important thing is to find the mine if there is one. These men are protecting something of importance. If that is not true, then I have no idea what the hell is going on."

"That's fine by me," the Major told Steve. "After having a briefing with my senior ranks. I would like to give it plenty of thought before I come back to you with a final plan of operation."

"Okay, Brian. At the moment we have spare time up our sleeve. We are secure and well guarded. But the sooner we start striking back at the opposition, the better." As it happened, that particular night was quiet.

Now the Major had some idea of what Benson required of him; he left Steve to go and brief his troops, to get this show on the road. He had two excellent junior officers, and three experienced sergeants to:. The military then took the rest of the day to come up with a plan of operation that Major Fawkner could take back to Steve the next morning.

In the barracks, the next morning Fawkner explained his plan of operations to Steve. When they were both in agreement, Steve called Sergeant Stephens come to the barrackroom office. To Stephens, Steve said, "I'm going to attach you and two more Mounties to the Major's group. You will be the liaison between the military and me as the RCMP Authority. If anyone needs arresting you or jimmy will do it. Not forgetting to read them their rights in every case. You should know the procedure now can you hadle that Sergeant Stephens.

"Not a problem Sir."

"Fine, go and pick two more men with winter experience to go with you, and then pack up your kit and report back here," Steve told the Sergeant. With the Major in tow, while they were waiting the two senior men went over the plan again to make sure nothing had been missed. As soon as he reported back, Steve and the Major, and the Sergeant with two men left to go to the Ranger HQ tent.

Steve wanted to say a few words to his men as well as the Rangers to impress on them the importance of what they were doing. He also wanted to impress on them that where possible to try and keep as many of the opposition alive. "Remember he told them, that you could not use dead bodies in a courtroom to point out the accused. At the same time, I am not sending you out there is a sacrifice your lives for the cause. Your safety is paramount in a shootout, beyond that I am not concerned, as validated is not you in the body bag. In other words do not take unnecessary risks."

CHAPTER 11

Back in the RCMP HQ in Ottawa, the better part of a week would pass and only after intense questioning would a small breakthrough be made. The RCMP interrogators realised that these men were initially recruited to operate a mine East of Fort good old in the shore of Great Bear Lake. The idea of a mine only came to light when they drop that he and some of his compatriots were hard rock miners.

Jimmy had been right when he said that the retreating opposition was travelling in a north-easterly direction. They were in fact, running towards the location of the mine to the East between Norman Wells or Fort Good Hope on the Western end of Great Bear Lake.

One of Moreau's ancestors had stumbled upon a small vein of gold near where the mine was now located, and more importantly they found five small to medium rough cut diamonds. A whole generation had passed before marauders uncle Henri bequeathed Moreau control of the construction business, because he had decided to spend more time and money and develop the mine site further. The following year it was left Moreau, because uncle Henri had died, before he had a chance to develop the mine further. It was Moreau who had taken up further development of the mine.

This was the current situation when Steve and his team became involved. Few of the company staff now working for Moreau knew of the existence of the mine. He intended to keep that status quo in place.

Now Steve's group were ready to start. The whole purpose of any action taken was to break up the opposition and to try and keep the mine open if there was one. Steve would be furious if the entrance to the mineshaft had been brought up to hide its presence. Talking to the Major Steve said, "Having said it once if there is no mine; what are they protecting? What have the choppers fly out of formation with one on each flank left and right to give a better view to Jimmy and the Sergeant."

"Come in from the Great Bear Lake, high enough to avoid any flak. With Jimmy and Sergeant Stephens as observers, they will look at this array differently. When you have passed over the area, swing away to the North and South before coming in for a second run. All I need is another of your choppers standing by over the lake area to bring my people hold if necessary. I will need to put in a report to our political Masters.

So after a quick explanation of the troops Steve withdrew back to the office." Before leaving the Major included his official photographer so the military and the RCMP could have a permanent aerial record.

Jimmy in the leading chopper said over the air for the benefit of the other flight crew, "below on my starboard side I can see what looks like the entrance to a mine. Come in slowly behind us and have a look. I will swing out wide and come back for another look." Jimmy's aircraft swung away in a wide arc and hovered to give the other machine space to look.

A short time later Sergeant Stephens came on air to say he also could see a mine entrance. Jimmy told him to swing out in a full arc and join his aircraft. Jimmy thought the mine entrance is not going anywhere so he had built coppers land near each other about a kilometre from the mine site. With a perimeter guard out for protection, Jimmy had the Sergeant and both pilots join him for a conflab.

"I would like to hit the mine now, but we must be careful not to get caught by a superior force. I'm going to call my boss now to find out what he would like is to do. I believe so far no one seems we pay any attention to us," Jimmy told them. "So let me call the boss and go from there."

"On air Jimmy said, "air to ground one are you receiving, over."

"Ground one at HQ receiving, over"

So as not to give too much away Jimmy said, "Two Bears calling. I require both seniors here with additional help in numbers. Have found what we are looking for. Opposition numbers are unknown. Will stand by our current position and wait for your arrival, we are at main grid square 25," Two Bears out.

"Ground one to air, message received and understood. Will join you ASAP. Ground one out."

Steve got hold of the Major, and told him to put a squad together to join them at the mine site. How quickly can you muster a team? I don't want to lose the element of surprise."

I have a team of 20 ready to move now. I set it up just in case it was needed for just such an exercise. Give the word ready when you are," the Major told him. To his 2IC the Major said, load the squad standing by at the moment, with everything needed for a firefight. Take the guard for this site just in case." With no time wasted the backup team was in the air in 15 minutes and on their way. Steve and the Major were in the leading chopper.

They came in behind the two aircraft on the ground. Jimmy and Stephens were standing by when Steve and the Major disembarked as the helicopter touched the snow. The Rangers quickly demanded and had their equipment sorted and ready to move in minutes. Jimmy spread out the map on the floor of the chopper. He pointed to the possible mine site and stood back so everyone could have a look.

"We are approximately one kilometre from the site. I think from this position we need to go in on foot."

Steve turned to the Major, "how long do you think it would take to go the distance in the present conditions."

"Half an hour to 40 minutes."

"Form three squads. One on each flank, we will go in with the middle squad for a frontal attack. Have two choppers stand-off to cover us from the air but wide enough to be outside rifle range. Enough let's get this show on the road.

The Rangers were quickly organised so they were on the move in 15 minutes. The ability to camouflage themselves in the snow they got to within 100 meters without being challenged. Steve said quietly into his radio Mike; everybody stand fast while the Major and I have a looksee." The two men made a slow approach one to either side of the entrance. Steve thought it strange that no one seemed to be guarding the mine. He was about to stand up when a shot was fired from inside the in his direction.

As soon as he heard the rifle fire, Steve and the Major hit the ground and moved away, so they were behind the rock face at the entrance. As soon as the two men were clear, the Rangers set a volley of rifle fire down the shaft of the mine. There were cries of anguish before a loud voice shouted, "We surrender, we are coming out now."

As soon as they were clear of the mine, the opposition was herded off to one side and told to lay down face down in the snow. Staying as low as possible a squad of Rangers inched their way into the mining before tossing in some flash bang grenades to roust out any opposition. There were immediate shouts of surrender. The remaining opposition was ordered to drag themselves out to the maintainers without weapons. Just to emphasise the point several Rangers fired a volley of rounds into the roof of the mine. Not enough to cause any real damage to the roof but enough to press home the point. Several stragglers came out of the entrance of the mine.

As soon as they were clear, they were herded off to one side be questioned about who remained in the main. Steve and the Major listened to the report before the Major told Steve he would head a squad to round of any other survivors. The two shots were fired at her direction, which caused one Ranger a flesh wound.

The Major in a raised voice shouted, "Open fire." Several volleys were sent down the mineshaft before the Major shouted, "Ceasefire." The Rangers moved further into the mine without any opposition. They found four wounded and several dead or dying. The Rangers quickly sorted out the bodies and swept the shaft to make sure there were no surprises left behind. What they did find in a remote corer was a makeshift grave that been disturbed by foraging animals.

Steve made sure it was safe before calling in Doctor Donna Connors to join them at the gravesite. He had three Mounties form a guard around Donna Major rabbit strict instructions from Steve what should happen if there is another attack. Donna enlisted the help of a couple of Marines to cover the before moving them to the mouth of the tunnel, where there was better light.

About the same time, a report came in the small RCMP barracks was under attack again. Steve told the Major to split his group in two quickly and return to base to make a sneak attack on the opposition from the rear. Steve was happy with the numbers left he should be safe for the time being. None the less, Steve had some of the remaining Rangers, form a perimeter guard outside about 300 meters from the entrance to the mineshaft. He ordered them to dig in to camouflage their existence.

Steve got hold of Jimmy for a quick talk.

"Benson here sir. Have no idea of the strength of the opposition. We are pinned down in the base building. I ordered our chopper to standoff. Till I hear from you, Benson standing by, out."

"Can you hold them till help gets there?

"Come in from the Great Bear Lake, high enough to avoid any flak. With Jimmy and Sergeant Stephens as observers, they will look at the terrain differently. When you have passed over the area, swing away to the north and south, before coming in for the second run. All I need is another of your choppers standing by over the lake area to bring my people home, if there is one available. I will need to put in a report to our political masters." With a quick agreement in place, the Ranger's choppers were off to carry out the recce. Before leaving, the Major included his official photographer so the military and the RCMP could have a permanent aerial record.

"Excellent DCS," the AC told him. "As you know the CC has given Carte Blanche to this operation, so you will not have any problems from the system. I will check on Armstrong from time to time to make sure he is not having any internal problems as well. I will act as his guardian angel. Other than that what can I do for you now?"

"Form three squads. One on each flank, we will go in with the middle squad for a frontal attack. Have two choppers standoff to cover us from the air, but wide enough to be outside rifle rage. Enough, let's get this show on the road."

"Have the map sectioned into grid squares. Give each section a grid reference and give me a copy, and make a rule that over the airwaves a grid reference number only is to be used, to confuse anyone listening out for our broadcasts. The only thing I can add is that Jimmy thinks that it must be northeast of Yellowknife in the same wilderness area were the remains of the Adams were found. If I fact, you do find a mine and you need to have someone arrested then I will send a RCMP Officer to make the arrest legal and to escort the prisoner back here. But I believe that we will have to take over control of the mine and hold it until our Political Masters decide the next step."

"Have you had any result concerning the two band guys who were keeping an eye on them?"

"Hold on Jimmy," Steve said while he passed on the information to AL about the two men Jimmy had caught watching what Jimmy and the rest were doing.

"Hold on Steve while I speak to the CC." Steve waited another ten minutes before the familiar voice of the CC came on line.

"I agree Steve. I will talk to the commissioner now and let you know what success I am having, ASAP. AC out." The AC returned the hadpiece to Jerry and left the office.

"I didn't hear that," the CC told Steve. "One thing I am going to do is to send you reinforcements, with all necessary equipment for an extended stay in the wilderness. I have already put this in motion, so the first of them should arrive early tomorrow. Our political bosses are reading the same page as us. You will in fact, have a force of almost two hundred both RCMP and Rangers under your command. You have bee appointed the Commandant in Charge. As the senior ranking officer, the word has been passed out that they are all to obey your commands in the field, no exceptions."

"I have a team of twenty ready to move now. I set it up just in case it was required for just such an exercise. Ready, when you are," the Major told him. To his 2IC the Major said, "Load the squad standing by at the moment, with everything needed for a firefight. Tighten the guard for this site just in case." With no time wasted, the backup team was in the air in fifteen minutes, and on their way. Steve and the Major were in the leading chopper.

"I have reopened the case of the young couple whose remains have just been discovered in the Northwest Territories south of Aylmer Lake. They had a home in Edmonton, so I was curious to know if you conducted an area canvas around their home address, and if so what was the result?"

"I have to warn you that I had Jerry put a super lock on the system to stop anyone getting into and altering ay of the files. I also had Jerry do a separate computer backup I case of a malfunction."

"I that, I agree DCS," the Commander said. "I will have everything covered from my end. We will be able to launch an emergency evacuation should the need arise."

"I will ignore that last remark; report back to me if you make any discoveries concerning this problem. AC over and out."

"I would like to hit the mine now, but we must be careful not to get caught by a superior force. I am going to call my boss now to find out what he would like us to do. I believe so far no one seems to be paying attention to us," Jimmy reported. "So let me call the boss and go from there."

"I'll come with you and have a word with Jimmy before you go. Do not worry if Jimmy goes out ahead and you think you might have lost him; do not waste time looking for him, he will find you. You can work out the details between you. Oh and he does out like formality just call him Jimmy. So let's get this show on the road," Steve said as he led the way outside.

"I'll let you get on with it so I can organize the airlift of your team. Talk to you soon, DCS. Yellowknife out."

"I'm going to call the boss to bring him up to date. First order of the day if they try to move, shoot them. If they ignore you, shoot to kill." For good measure, Jimmy fired several shots in the air. Jimmy walked further away keeping the group in sight, regardless. When he had Steve on air, he quickly explained the situation.

"I'm requesting that you keep them under lock and key as long as you can. Although I find it strange that these two have not as yet asked for a lawyer."

"If the band guys launch a concerted attack, DS Two Bears will be able to hold them off, depending on the strength of the attack until you send help. He will set up a camp perimeter that lets him guard all sides. Can you have an operator listen out for DS Two Bears? I am not worried about him; I am concerned about the two females because one of them is a forensic pathologist. The troopers can look after themselves."

"If you could spring the use of a chopper, I would like Sergeant Stephens and me to go out at first light to do a recce from the air," Jimmy told Steve.

"It does from the point of view that it is another unsolved murder," Steve told her. "The phone here must surely be working?" Picking up the phone, Steve dialled the umber for his office. On the third ring, a familiar voice said 'Cold case squad, DS Armstrong speaking."

"Jerry try to set up a phone link connection between you and me and the senior RCMP officer in Edmonton. If you manage it, before you connect me, make sure you of the gender and rank of the Commandant, so I do not say the wrong thing of calling my office and wait till you call me."

"Jill I want you to man the base here. Order of the Day contact Jerry back at HQ and ask him to set up a direct link between himself and you here, using a laptop computer so that information is logged directly into our system. We are going to lose some of the information if we do not start getting it into our system. I need you to do this Jill as you are apart from Jerry, are our most competent computer operator."

"Jill," Steve said, "How would you like a trip to the northwest for a bit of adventure?"

"Jimmy fire a couple of rounds over their heads every now and then to keep them in line," Steve told Jimmy. Fortunately, the chopper was there within thirty minutes. It arrived just as more bad guys decided to attack the base hut.

"Jimmy, you, Stephens and Jim Henry go out quietly and do a recce, one left and right and you in the middle Jimmy. Get your heads together and decide how you wat to cover the area. If you happen to find anyone, arrest him or her, and drag them back here. Off you go." Steve ordered.

"Lt. Bowes I want you under DI. Al Philips to use your men and ours to lay out a base for a tented camp for the additional incoming troops that are on their way. They will also bring extra equipment whether we use it or out. Draw up a guard roster to act as snow bunnies in the heavy winter clothing we already have. I want them to disappear into the scenery; I am sure I do not have to spell it out for you. This is to be put in motion immediately. Al get hold of Jimmy Two Bears, a First Nation Tribal Chief, and introduce him to our friend here. Lt. Bowes I want you to take whatever advice Jimmy suggests because he is a wilderness survival expert. Off the you go and get started; I'll wait for the rest of the additional incoming troops to arrive."

"Message received and understood Air 1 out."

"No boss, I don't think so."

"Not a problem, sir."

"Nothing boss, I just wanted you brought up to date. On that note, I will get on with it. Benson over and out."

"Now it is time to tackle the other problem of the death of the politician Gregory Stains. How many men have you got remaining?"

"Ok chief. I'll let you know what cases we decide to unravel."

"Right I'm going to remain here; I want you to take two helicopters and the men and go to this location that Jimmy has marked on the map. Flush out any stragglers and if the cabin happens to be destroyed in the process, the so be it. Sergeant Stephens, you stay, Jimmy you go to make sure we are attacking the right building. Leave now."

"Okay let's get this show on the road," Steve told them.

"Let's see if we can't get some information from this rat. Who are you and why are you here," Jimmy asked the man. With no answer forthcoming, Jimmy fired a round from his revolver close to man's ear.

"Okay, Brian. at the moment, we have spare time up our sleeve. We are secure and well-guarded. But the sooner we start striking back at the opposition, the better." As it happened, that particular night was quiet.

"Okay, Jerry get on with finding out about Stains' past. I will try to bring as much pressure to bear as possible from the CC if I can. When you have caught up with that, do the same for the young couple Séan and Sally Adams whose remains were discovered south of Aylmer Lake, north of Reliance, NWT. Look for a possible link to Stains or Moreau, maybe that is the answer, Benson out."

"Okay, Major put a squad together and let's go join them at the mine site. How quickly can you muster a team? I don't want to lose the element of surprise."

"On that note, I'll get on with it. Benson out."

"Once we establish the link between all the main characters, I will get on with making a criminal prosecution. We will have to be careful because Politicians will be involved. At the same time, we need to be prudent and put in place laws that will not allow this to happen again. All Major family Trust funds over a set amount will need to be investigated for any criminal activities. The Attorney General, on behalf of the Government, will need to set the amount of the starting dollar value of any Trust under observation. So that we the RCMP can go ahead without interference from Family Trust members or accountants and the legal profession." Steve told his boss.

"Sir I believe that this group of bandits was waiting in ambush solely to keep people out of the area. However, at this point, I have no idea what it was that they were protecting. Until we do find the reason, we cannot go forward. It has to have something to do with mining for gold or oil, or more importantly raw diamonds, that someone might be mining illegally on Crown Land, or land under the control of First Nations.

The silence was disturbed by the muffled sound of long guns being fired in their direction.

"That came from the direction of one the guard positions." Al pointed out. On air, Al said, "This is #2 have we been attacked or not, all guards report their status."

"That is a lofty approach, but you are correct. I will take it up with the CC and let you know the outcome. For now, carry o regardless."

"That is a relieve DCS. But where does that leave us?"

"That's all fine by me, Steve. I will go and have a briefing with my senior ranks. I would like to give it plenty of thought before I come back to you with the final plan of operation."

"That's it, Barry you head for the camp. Make sure they are in an area they can defend and bring back a snowmobile and trailer so we can get these two back to base."

"The more I think about this, the more I'm convinced that there is a definite link between Stains, Reynolds, Moreau, and the Adams. I want you to do a-depth study of the Stains family history, and the history of the Adams family tree as well. Find me a link no matter how tenuous," Steve told Jerry.

"Start the recorder for this." Steve waited for Jerry to tell him, he was being recorded before giving an in-depth report on events to date. When he finished, he told Jerry to have a look at every aspect of the history of Gregory Stains. There has to be a connection, which leads up to the present. "Ignore everything else this has total priority."

"This is up to you," Jimmy said. "Do you have enough fuel for us to do a recce to both these places? If you have, we could have a look-see. However, you would need to swig out wide, so the opposition does not know we are on to them. We might find the mining camp they are using as a base. You would have cameras on board so we could get some aerial photos to take back. Then I would like you to backtrack along the same route back to Wrigley. I would like to take them by surprise if possible."

"Understand, rescue is on the way," Yellowknife out.

"Up the proverbial creek. What I need from you is for me to have total access so I can rammish around in Government archives to try and find the answer as to why somebody is still interested in what happened to Stains after all this time."

"Very wise Steve, whatever I have nothing for you. With all checks and balances in place have Jerry call me about this subject?"

"We are approximately one klm from the site. I think from this position we need to go in on foot."

"We have now taken out twenty seven of the opposition counting dead or wounded. The area around the mine is now under our control, and the mine should not give us any more problems. I have left a squad of an officer, a sergeant and twenty men as a guard. That of course will be bolstered tomorrow with tribal volunteers, now everything is quiet. Nevertheless, we must keep our vigilance strong regardless.

"When we first got attacked it was from this quarter. Using Jimmy Two Bears' superior tracking skills, I would like you to swig out in a full arc to see if you can cut across the direction the attackers took either coming or going. With a bit of luck, we could track them to their lair before we bring in the heavy equipment. It is up to you, but if you could pick a team of ten men with hard experience in the frozen north adequately equipped for winter warfare, we could maybe shorten this engagement."

"Yes and no. We are sorting through the details. All we have managed to gain so far is the fact that a large mining company employs them as security advisers."

"Yes boss," Jerry told Steve, "It appears that Stains has lived in Yellowknife, Wrigley, and Fort Providence. His family line goes back almost to the begining of Canada's history. His family still have business interests across the North West Territories."

"Yes, boss, message understood, over and out."

"Yes, that is a question we must have answered sooner rather than later, DCS."

"You know your men better than me. I would like you to come up with a plan to use your Rangers to search the area for an ore mine. It most likely will have an abandoned look as a disguise."

A crime syndicate who were striving to control all the gold and diamonds unearthed in the Northwest Territories had instigated this whole scenario. They could have got away with this crime, except for the fact that Stains was a member of the legislative council. In addition, from that standpoint, his death would not go noticed. There was also the considerable pressure brought to bear by the Stains family. Senior police knew that because of his status in the community they would not be allowed to treat his death and disappearance as a casual event. As a cold case, it would stay on the books until brought to a satisfactory conclusion.

A few minutes after the AC left "I suppose I better try and make peace with AC," Steve said as he went towards his office. Once seated he picked up his phone and dialled the AC's office. "Benson here sir, I apologize for my earlier remarks, no offense intended. I did not get to ask if you had any more odd cases floating around. I am about to start reviewing the cold case file ow that Jerry has sorted all the team reports into the system?"

A local business owner who was to take him to the meeting with Reynolds picked up Stains from his guesthouse the morning of his death. Stains found two other men were waiting in the limo when he got in. The driver took them to a spot north of Wrigley, where they wanted Stains to inspect a prospecting claim, which the First Nations had claimed was on their land. The area was a three-square kilometre piece of scrubland northeast of Wrigley, close to Keller Lake. Stains had to walk the last half kilometre to get there. When the small group was sufficiently off the beaten track, one of the men hit Stains on the back of the head with a piece of iron bar. Stains was dead before he hit the ground. The murderers made sure he was dead before picking up his body and throwing it into a hollow in the ground. Then they covered him with loose soil. Satisfied that it would be a long time before or if anyone found the remains.

A short time later Sergeant Stephens came on air to say, he also could see a mine entrance. Jimmy told him to swig out in a full arc and join his aircraft. Jimmy thought the mine is not going anywhere so he have both helicopters land near each other, about a kilometer from the mine site. With a perimeter guard out for protection, Jimmy had Sergeant Stephens and both pilots join him for a conflab.

About late morning, Jimmy was thinking of calling a lunch break when he had the sensation of being watched. All four were sitting on logs in a slight hollow when Jimmy said quietly, "I want you two ladies to keep on talking about some of the articles we've found so far, try and get a little friendly argument going. I have the feeling we are being watched.

About the same time, a report came in that the small RCMP barracks was under attack. Steve told the Major to split his group in two quickly and return to base to make a sneak attack on the opposition from the rear. Steve was happy that with the umbers left he should be safe enough for the time being. None the less, Steve had some of the remaining Rangers form a perimeter guard outside about 300 meters from the entrance to the mineshaft. He ordered them to dig in, to camouflage their existence.

According to the Parliamentary file, this was a scheduled visit, so there should have been nothing out of the ordinary. Unfortunately, Stains went off the air, and not even his remains had been located to Date. Assuming he had been murdered and not gone missing deliberately. It was also reported that one of the people he met with at the time, Tom Reynolds, a local small businessperson, also disappeared just over a month later. The two facts might be unrelated. I would still flag them as liked together. When Reynolds disappeared, it was still too soon after the disappearance of Stains. Therefore the two events had to be tied together."

After a quick study of Stains' itinerary, Jerry passed it on to Steve. Steve also had a good look before giving it to Al Philips, his 2 IC. Stains' agenda did not allow for time wasting, so he would have been busy up to the time he disappeared. The purpose of Stains' visit was to sort out some problems the local First Nations were having regarding boundary lines and prospecting. Stains had elected to be based mainly in Wrigley, on the Mackenzie River.

After the usual pleasantries, Moreau said, "You will be flying to the edge of the Arctic Circle. The first thing I want you to do is to assemble the winter survival gear and get it stowed aboard the chopper. You might have to camp out so make sure you are carrying tents and sleeping bags. You know what is needed; off you go now and report when you are ready to leave."

After Thompson made a report of the latest catastrophe regarding the mine, Moreau decided that they had better get their stories straight, now they had the RCMP and the Rangers howling for their blood.

Again, it was not only the unearthing of the link between the main characters, that Jerry found, it was putting it all together that made the difference. That would come about with input from the whole team. It was evident that Steve Benson had a flair for extracting the best endeavours from everyone.

Al and Jimmy moved out first leaving the others to watch their backs. Jimmy was the first to find the one person left behind. He was dead from being struck by at least two bullets in the area of his chest. Jimmy reported the fact to Steve over the radio.

Al was just about to leave when Sergeant Stephens arrived. "You made good time getting here. I want you to have a look at what we have found. Then I want you to relieve the trooper guarding the way here. I want to question him on how he found the gravesite. Once I have a few answers, I wat you to remain here. I will seed two more troopers because I want this burial site protected against all comers. Standing order of the Day is I want you to arrest anyone who comes within rifle range. When I have all the information I can extract, and Dr. Connors our pathologist has examined the area, I will have the remains, and the rest of you moved back to the RCMP base. When DS Two Bears arrives, I want you to be his assistant. This light snowfall is a pain, and it may have already obliterated any sign on the ground, but we have to try."

All guard positions indicated clear accept Joe Bascal. Joe reported that he had discovered he was under watch by persons unknown, so he fired in that direction and was rewarded by the sound of a snowmobile moving away. To protect himself as soon as he shot at the opposition, he changed his position so they could not do a Jimmy and return fire to his location. All he could report was that he found no trace of the opposition when he got to the approximate position of the other person.

Apart from all this when Gregory had recruited Sean & Sally Adams; it was to give him more ammunition for when he fronted Moreau his uncle about the disappearance of some of the company fortune. To this end, he offered to fund the Adams wedding, if they agreed to postpone their honeymoon to the later date. In addition, he had them agree to have it in the frozen north. He had carefully explained the reasons about how he thought Moreau was siphoning off raw diamonds and profits. Gregory also told them he would supply the latest survival gear, including an up to Date snowmobile and trailer of the kind needed for man to operate in comfort in extreme weather conditions. The Adams were more than happy to follow

Gregory's plan to unseat Moreau as head of the company, and the Family Trust.

As Jerry took up the challenge, Moreau was getting a report from Joe Thompson. What Thompson had to tell him was not good news. Jerry trawling police records discovered that Thompson had not been a good boy. He had a long string of charges against him some of which had yet to be brought to court. There was no doubt that Thompson was a standover man and a criminal of the first order. Going through Thompson's history, Jerry could not understand why Thompson was not rotting in some prison. It had to be that he had friends in high places, or was owed many payback favours.

As soon as they heard the rifle fire, Steve and the Major hit the ground and moved away, so they were behind the rock face at the entrance. As soon as the two men were clear, the Rangers set a volley of rifle fire down the shaft of the mine. There were cries of aguish before a loud voice shouted, "We surrender, and we are coming out ow."

As soon as they were clear of the mine, they were herded off to one side and told to lay face down in the snow. Staying as low as possible a squad of Rangers inched their way into the mine before tossing in some flash-bag grenades to roust out any opposition. There were shouts of surrender. The remaining opposition were ordered by loudhailer to drag themselves out to the entrance without weapons. Just to emphasize the point, the Rangers fired a volley of rounds into the roof of the mine. Not enough to cause any real damage to the roof but enough to press home the point. Several stragglers made their way to the entrance of the mine.

As soon as they were clear, they were also herded off to one side to be questioned about who remained in the mine. Steve and the Major listened to the report before the Major told Steve he would head a squad to round up any other survivors. The Major had his men hug the walls on either side of the shaft, while they kept as low a profile as possible. Two shots were fired in their direction, which caused one Ranger a flesh wound to the side of his face. The Major in a raised voice shouted, "Open fire." Several volleys were set down the mineshaft before the Major shouted "Ceasefire." The Rangers moved further into the mine without any opposition. They found four wounded and several dead or dying. The Rangers quickly sorted out the bodies and swept the shaft to make sure there were no surprises left behind. What they did find in a remote corer was a makeshift grave that been disturbed by foraging animals.

At the QM's store, introductions were made all around. Gibbs looked to be very fit, with a demeanour that suggested he could hadle himself regardless of the situation. Forbes was a grizzled old-timer who looked like he had just stepped out of a page of the RCMP history book.

At the same time, Donna sat in one of the small rooms reading the forensic reports of both cases. She sat there thinking that there is not going to be any direction to come from the DA reports, and DA would have only been a backup anyway. Donna thought, 'I might in fact, need to go and cover the same ground where the young couples' remains were found to make sure that nothing of importance was left behind.' To do that she would need the experienced eyes of Jimmy Two Bears along because he was so very good at reading sign. She went out into the main room to talk to Steve. Jerry told her that Steve was in his office talking to the commandant in Edmonton. "Donna can it wait till Steve has finished?"

At Wrigley base, it was easier for Donna to give a more accurate conclusion to a DA report on the skeletal remains. "I am very confident that this was Stains," Donna told Steve, but does that help you at all knowing that fact?"

Back at the base, with the AC on a secure lie, Steve explained what he had done so far. "I believe it was prudent to let the local First Nations shoulder their end of the bargain. That will leave my small force, and the military unit, to get on with ending this event. I do not want to waste more time than necessary.

Back in the RCMP HQ in Ottawa, the better part of a week would pass, and only after intense interrogation, would there be a breakthrough. The RCMP interrogators realized that these men were recruited initially to operate a mine to the northeast of Yellowknife. This was in a wilderness area. The idea of a mine became known when one man let it drop that he and some of his compatriots were hard rock miners.

Barry had done the same to the other man.

Barry was back in no time. He and Jimmy picked up the two would be assassins and dumped them in the trailer. Jimmy made sure the two me were out of earshot before making the radio call to Yellowknife. With the senior officer on the line, Jimmy gave a quick explanation and the fact that he wanted the two would be assassins airlifted back to Yellowknife for interviewing and charging if necessary. The chopper was there within the hour with extra hads to escort the prisoners back to Yellowknife. A senior officer also came to make sure Jimmy and his small squad were not under threat of any kid. Satisfied he left promising Jimmy to let him know if any usable Intel was the outcome.

Before Gregory Stains had gone on his ill-fated tour he had recruited his nephew and soon to be niece, Sean and Sally Adams. He first talked them into delaying their honeymoon by offering to pay all their wedding expenses. He wanted them to take a cold trip to the North West fully equipped with the latest gear to survive north of the Arctic Circle, including log-rage radio communication. He wanted them to camp in an area close to the site of the other family mine, which was producing some quality raw diamonds. Gregory had wanted them to remain in that area for at least two weeks to observe and report to him.

Before moving out, Steve made sure Donna was wearing her bulletproof vest. Then throwing caution to the wide, he made the gesture with his arm to go so they could get to the gravesite as quickly as possible.

By ten o'clock mid-morning, they were onsite ready to go. The chopper was big enough to carry the other snowmobiles and two trailers, and some extra fuel, packed aboard one of them. One of the officers who had come with them showed Jimmy where the remains were found. As it was a bright cloudless Day Jimmy picked out a campsite, and with the extra hads, the camp was set up in no time.

Captain Dixon, the aerial commander, called Wrigley base. "Air one calling ground one."

Donna had removed the rest of the snow covering the remains so she could go to work. When she had extracted as much information as could be had from the area, Steve ordered them to pack up ready to head back to base. Under Donna's direction, the body remains were carefully picked up, placed in one of the trailers, and covered by a small tarp, now Donna was the ready to go. Steve gave the order to move out. He had Al lead, and Jimmy bring up the rear with himself in the middle. They wasted no time returning to base.

Donna was almost finished doing a DNA profile on the body remains, when two shots were fired at her position. Steve had made sure she would not be in a situation where she could be attacked directly. He was off to one side and picked up the approximate position of the shooter or shooters. He fired six rounds rapidly at that area. One of the others did the same thing, and they were rewarded by the sound of what could have been a death cry.

Due to the time lapse from when Stains died and the present, a lot of time had been lost, so the trail was also long dead when Benson eventually became involved in the investigation. Steve was going to have to look at every aspect of Stains' life no matter how minute to try to draw a lie across that life that was Gregory Stains. The primary complaint of Stains' constitutes was the fact the quality of gold when assayed was not the same gold that was offered for sale later. Stains knew that the only way to prove this was true was to try to follow a small amount of gold from the mine to the product in the jeweller's shop, or government storage. Unfortunately, this could not be said of the diamonds as well. Discoveries of gold and diamonds in the area was a magnet for the criminal underworld.

Everybody was up at first light. The two girls got breakfast going, while the men started packing up the trailers with the tents and equipment. It took about an hour and a half, and they were on their way south. In spite of snow falling, they made good time. Jimmy intended to keep going as long as he could before calling a halt for a meal break.

From the list of outstanding cases to solve, these were two cases suggested for investigation, one by AL Philips and the other by Jerry Armstrong. One from a detective's point of view and one from a computer analyst's point of view. The two cases picked out, also had newspaper reports attached, all of which Jerry had set to Steve's computer. Steve sat there going over these statements while the rest made some sense out of the original investigation of the death of a young newly married couple conducted but abandoned ad declared open/unsolved. On the surface, they both looked to be difficult and would take a lot of hard work, but that was the point of the exercise.

Gregory Stains accidentally came across more activities that were suspicious when he arranged to talk to Tom Reynolds who ran a small business on the fringe of the large mining companies. Reynolds was under the misapprehension that Gregory was part of the conspiracy, when he arranged to meet with the politician about his cut from any illegal diamonds mined. His complaint was his cut, which was getting smaller each time. Gregory had made a pledge to make another visit to the NWT to talk to Reynolds, first before seeing his uncle. Having some, but not all of the plot, Gregory unfortunately confronted his uncle about this. By telling him he would get the whole story from Reynolds when he next visited the Northwest Territories. However, the die was cast, by broaching the subject with Moreau; he had signed his own death warrant.

His secretary left to get on with the task of finding Joe Thompson. Thompson was the chief trouble-shooter for Moreau. Whenever there was a problem concerning a work dispute or to settle a labour dispute,

Thompson would go in every time to resolve matters. It took the better part of forty minutes to find Thompson. When Grace got Thompson on the line, she told him, "He requires your presence here urgently, Joe."

However, this plan of action also sealed the fate of the young couple, the Adams, when Moreau had them executed and buried in a remote area. With their belongings scattered over a wide area never to be found. Their remains would in fact be found eventually leading to Steve Benson bringing charges against the people responsible. Their snowmobile registration was charged and the boss of Moreau's killing squad claimed it as his ow. So all of that passed into history.

In an attempt to protect themselves when they moved Steve told his men and the shooters in the base hut to take the Majority down either dead or wounded. The two remaining lifted their arms in surrender after putting their weapons on the ground. Steve and his team had them cable tied up and on the ground in minutes. Steve made sure that he had all of their mouths taped so they could not shout out a warning to the rest. He was not worried about the dead, and the living would be seen to, when they had this situation under control.

I fact, all six had passed the course.

I fact, the mining company that employed the attackers, sent to harass Steve and anybody who showed an interest, were employed by the Lost Hope Mine, owed by the Stains Family Trust and under the control of Séan Louis Moreau, a uncle of the politician Gregory Stains. The mine was located northeast of Yellowknife in a remote area off the beaten track. Moreau was well aware of the fact that his uncle had come across the deposits of gold and raw diamonds by accident. He had kept the location secret only having it passed on to his nephew when he died.

As regards the search for Gregory Stains, and in spite of calling in volunteers, additional RCMP officers, and the State rescue service no trace of Stains was found. Due to the fact of Stains' official status in the Government, the current Grosvenor of the NWT kept the search going for a month, with no result. Immediately after the search was terminated the file was marked open-unsolved and sent to the RCMP HQ with a copy to the Government Archives.

In keeping with what Jerry had sent, Steve and Al used the information to divide the local map into grid squares for the search. As soon as the maps were finished each searcher was given a copy and sent on their way, it was at least keeping them occupied. One of the primary thigs Steve was hoping that they would find an obscure mine not registered on government maps. What he would find later was the fact that the second mine, the one that Moreau was stealing from, was further anyway. Twenty minutes after that one of the searchers called base on the two-way radio.

In no time, the firing from the opposition became less against the sound of departing snowmobiles. The military had already split to form a pincer movement and was moving in for a more direct attack. With one last push, they walked into the where the enemy position had been. They found several dead and wounded. The wounded were quickly rounded up and searched for ID's, and hidden weapons they have been carrying as well. In addition, they were made to sit in a group. Donna as the resident doctor checked all the dead to make sure there were no signs of life. The military had brought body bags as a precaution, so the Major selected a small group under a sergeant to put the bodies into the body bags and line them up along the sidewall of the RCMP barracks. Due to the low temperature, leaving them outside was equal to putting the remains into a refrigerator.

In the barracks, the next morning Fawkner explained his plan of operation to Steve. When they were both I agreement, Steve called Sergeant Stephens to come to the barracks. To Stephens, Steve said, "I am going to attach you and two more Mounties to the Major's group. You will be the liaison between the Military and me as the RCMP Authority. If anyone needs arresting, you will do it. Not forgetting to read them their rights in every case. You should know the procedure. Now can you hadle that Sergeant Stephens?"

In the early days of being give control of the mine, Moreau, and Thompson, after spending several days doing a complete survey of the mine operation, found the hiding place for the blood diamonds. That Moreau's uncle left them behind when he died. There were several stones some large some small. The first thig to do was to have them assayed, but quietly. He already had two silent partners that fitted the bill. Gregory Stains, Politician, and Tom Reynolds, a local small business owner, a known associate of Stains who was also a licensed precious mineral-chartered surveyor.

In the middle of all this, Steve had Jimmy go out a couple of kilometres, accompanied by Stephens the other RCMP sergeant to see if he could track the band guys. They were back in 3 hours to report that as long as it did not, snow they could maybe have some success. There was no doubt the opposition had gone off in a north easterly direction. Therefore, with a bit of caution, they could follow behind them.

They found a hunter's hut, it was unmanned, but they moved in any way and set themselves up for the night. Between them, they had a fire going and a meal cooking. Jimmy was glad they were off the trail with a roof over their heads. Jimmy called Jerry back at base to report their current position and the fact everyone was in good health.

It took the better part of two hours before the chopper returned. Jimmy did not waste time he had his map folded to pinpoint the location of what he thought was a large log cabin cover by snow and disguised by the surrounding bushland.

It was a hard ride back to base, due to the wind forming small snowdrifts, but Steve still made it in with time to spare. Once inside the small barracks, Steve did not stop to take off his outer storm gear. He picked up the radio mike and put out the call sig for the RCMP Base, at Yellowknife. When the operator answered his call, Steve identified himself and told the man at the other end to put him through to the Commandant immediately.

It was just as well as Steve's group had sustained minor casualties and were getting low on ammo.

It was love at first sight when Moreau and Thompson first met. It was a case of recognizing a fellow criminal. What cemented the partnership was the first murder they carried out together, that of a small construction boss that argued about fair compensation for work done. It was when the contractor threatened to take Moreau to the Court of Arbitration that the decision to eliminate him from the scene permanently was made.

It was several hours before Reynolds reported the absence of Stains to authorities, and unfortunately, some time elapsed before an official search was organized and put in place.

It was the fact that the Adams sustained a brutal attack that destroyed their facial features so it would be difficult to identify them later. Donna Connors would find some of the answers when she did another forensic study of their skeletal remains. Of course what makes it difficult for police investigators around the world is collecting enough evident quickly enough to first indentify and then arrest the perpetrators before taking them to court to have them sentenced and locked up for a very long time. Steve Benson would make sure that Moreau would have his Day in court, from which point he would never see light of Day again.

It would be some days before Jerry called his boss with a result.

Jack Armstrong, Jim Henry, and Joe Bascal. Remember this exercise involves a politician, Gregory Stains, who has been missing for some time presumed deceased.

Jerry cut in saying he had three seats available for a flight to Yellowknife, with a helicopter standing by to take them to the search area.

Jerry had already rearranged the possible list of cases to tackle. Steve had had the team do an in-depth study of the cases listed, which he had extracted from the unsolved list he had first suggested. Steve's, only worry was keeping everyone's feet of the ground and focused on the task. Steve was well aware that concluding the First Nation's Incident had been no easy task.

Jerry had also extracted the names and rank of the senior investigators. A DCI Alex Henderson and a DI Phil Hughes.

Jerry thought, 'why am I always left in charge when there is only me, to be in charge off?'

Jerry was still waiting for the Parliamentary Secretary to supply him with the itinerary for Stains' visit to the Northwest Territories. Jerry was about to make another request when the route was posted to his electronic mail system. Now they had a starting point. The trouble might be the fact that Stains' visit was several hundred km's from where Jimmy and the two girls were operating, which meant that the team would be spread over a significant portion of the NWT. Steve knew he would have to rely on the good graces of the AC for more help if it became necessary. Steve was confident that if meant more significant unsolved cases were cleared off the books that the AC would give Steve any additional aid he needed.

Jimmy and Barry slipped away like shadows, one left one right, to do a recce of the area, while the girls kept up the pretence of an argument over what had been found. Barry came across two men who had the camp under surveillance. He gave a birdcall that he knew Jimmy would respond to while keeping a strict watch on the two men.

Jimmy and his little band said their goodbyes and the helicopter was off back to base. The first thing Jimmy did as soon as they left was a radio check; everything was fine. He got a fire and coffee going so he could talk to the two girls.

Jimmy and his two companions moved out like shadows. The Sergeant found a bunch of three men that looked to be laying up in ambush. It seemed as if they were waiting for Steve and his men to come searching for them. The sergeant gave the bird whistle agreed to as meaning come to my position. He kept bird whistling until the other two made had caught up with him, they were back in their allotted position. The order of the day was, try to bring them in alive if possible.

Jimmy fired his gun again just nicking the man's ear, who let out a yell, and started to blubber.

Jimmy fired two shots over the heads of the attackers and in a voice from the other side of grave said aloud, "Surrender now or be sent to hell. You are under attack by a superior force. Show yourself if you wish to live."

Jimmy had been right when he said that the retreating opposition was traveling in a north easterly direction. They were in fact, running towards the location of a mine to the east between the Great Bear Lake, which was owned and operated by the Stains Family Trust.

In the led chopper, Jimmy said over the air for the benefit of the other flight crew, "Below on my starboard side I can see what looks like the entrance to a mine. Come in slowly behind us to have a look. I will swing out wide and come back for another look." Jimmy's aircraft swung out in a wide arc and hovered to give the other machine space to look.

Jimmy made sure they carried their firearms with them at all times. Jill kept thinking that Jimmy was so methodical the way he went about everything. She did not feel intimidated by her surroundings and the fact that they were in a wilderness area, having Jimmy Two Bears in charge. It was also the way Jimmy insisted they leave behind no rubbish.

Jimmy sidled up to Barry and made a gesture for Barry to come in behind the man on the left while Jimmy came up behind the man on the right. In a voice that sounded like it came from the grave, Jimmy said, "Put your weapons down slowly and raise your hads.

Jimmy tossed a coin for heads or tails and asked the pilot to pick. The pilot chose heads, which turned up. "Okay pick the group you want to follow, and off you go, but mark this spot on your map. We will probably have to fly over the other track at some time."

Just then, Jerry interrupted Steve to tell him the AC had just walked in. "Good Jerry put him on the lie."

Just to confuse things a bit more, Steve had broken down the search area into west and east. Starting at the top end of the search area, the first western grid square was designated number one, and the first eastern square number two, and so on in that order. With the squares of approximate size to each other, and numbered using every other number. That put grid square number 14 near the bottom of the east side

Knowing his boss would not want to waste any time Jerry had gone ahead and booked the flights and accommodation, "Already done boss."

Nevertheless, some of the information had filtered back to be lodged in company records, it was Jerry Armstrong who would unearth this fact. Steve had Jerry go on a slightly different tract to look for any equipment Stains had supplied to the Adams for their journey north. Jerry eventually unearthed the list of equipment including the snowmobile and trailer. The snowmobile would also prove to be essential evidence when Moreau's chief henchman, Thompson, appeared in court, to be given the same sentence as his boss. However, all of this to come later.

None the less, Steve was glad when the prisoners were off his hads. It was time to draw up the plan of operations with the Major. As a starting point, the first job was to try to find this mysterious mine, if in fact one excited. He was not short of helpers; he had enough men to search a large area. Considering they had survival clothing and snowmobiles the task should not be too difficult, as long as they were not under attack.

Now Steve's group were ready to start to try to unravel the corporate mess of the Stains Family Trust. The whole purpose of any action was to break the opposition's control and try to keep the mine open if there is one. Steve would be furious if the entrance to the mine shaft has been blow up to hide its presence. Talking to the Rangers senior officer in charge, Steve said, "Having said it once, I will say it again, if there is no mine; what are they protecting? What I want you to do is to approach the area from the direction of Great Bear Lake. Have the choppers fly out of formation with one on each flak left and right, to give a better view to Jimmy and the other RCMP sergeant."

Now that Steve Benson with the help of the Rangers had control of the mine, he arranged to have roving patrols to try and cut off any attack that could occur. He also put in place a rule that if the weather turned nasty, the patrols should spend only an hour and a half on patrol. It was one of these patrols that found another unmarked gravesite containing body remains, which had been disturbed by scavengers. When the patrol reported the find, Steve had them stand by to wait for Dr. Donna and Jimmy to have a look. While Donna was doing her thing, Jimmy with the four Mounties Steve had sent with him accompanied Jimmy on a walkabout looking for any sign. Unfortunately, if there had been any sign it had long been eliminated.

Now the Major had some idea what Benson required of him; he left Steve to go and brief his troops, to get this show on the road. He had two excellent junior officers, and three experienced sergeants to call o. The military took the rest of the day to come up with a plan of operation that Major Fawkner could take back to Steve the next morning.

Now with the formalities over the two senior ranks went inside the small RCMP barracks. "Let's get rid of the formalities; you can call me boss or Steve whichever is easier."

On air, Steve said, "This is #1. I will hold my position. The rest of you using caution move to where you think the shooters were hiding."

On the other had, Moreau in spite of a lack of business expertise had taken the company passed the point where it was when he was handed the rains. The problem was that Moreau believed that you had to break all the rules to win. That was true of the Lost Hope mine. It was on land that was under control of the First Nations. That was why Thompson, Moreau's roustabout, had initially recruited eighty-five miners from the oil and mining industries to work the mine and for security when required. The miners built two log cabins for accommodation disguised enough to make them appear to be part of the landscape. Some of the men were hunters and trappers so that they could supply themselves with fresh meat and fish in abundance.

Once again, Séan Louis Moreau had won the Day and survived to carry on, on his merry way. It was the constant attention, paid to all information by DS Jerry Armstrong, who would uncover the link between Gregory Stains and the young couple Sea & Sally Adams. This would give his boss Steve Benson the ability to link it all together. I the end, Benson would build a case that Séan Louis Moreau's lawyers could not fracture. However, this would happen in time, or a time long enough for Séan Louis Moreau to become comfortable with the fact he believed he was above the law.

Once on the ground, Jimmy had the pilot climb down so he could discuss what they were doing next. With the map spread out on the floor of the chopper Jimmy told the pilot that he believed the opposition were travelling in the direction of Norman Wells or Fort Good Hope.

Once Stains and Reynolds had expressed their glee that there would be diamonds to share, they had to be eliminated quickly and quietly, but only after, they rendered their report on the diamonds. Moreau did not intend to share with anyone what was produced by the mine. As much as Thompson was useful Moreau would not think twice about killing Thompson, it was the difference between the quick and the dead.

Once Steve gave Jerry Armstrong, the word that he had the backing of the AC, "In other words don't brook any interference from anyone until you have whatever information is available," Steve told Jerry. "The problem is that area commanders whatever their rank, believed they had the last word, so play the AC card when necessary."

One of Gregory's priorities of his visit to the territories was to check on the company assets. Some of the family Trust members were not happy with the way the company was being managed. Séan Louis Moreau was also the current managing director and CEO of all the company assets of the Stains Family Trust. More importantly, he was head of a small crime syndicate; he set up to try to gain control of any small mining ventures in the same area that were extracting rough diamonds. Gregory Stains was searching for any anomaly out of the ordinary Day-to-Day activities, which would show if his uncle was siphoning off profits before they were declared in the monthly balance of the company's profit and loss statement.

One of Séan Moreau's ancestors, his mother's brother, had stumbled upon a small vein of gold near where the mine was now located, and more importantly, they found five small to medium rough-cut diamonds. A whole generation had passed before Moreau's uncle Henry who had bequeathed him the construction business decided to spend more time and money and develop the mine site further. He uncovered both gold and uranium deposits close to one another. Unfortunately, he died early the following year, which eventually meant that it was bequeathed to Séan Moreau to take up further development of the mine. This was the current situation when Steve and his team became involved. Few of the company staff now working for Moreau knew of the existence of the mine. He intended to keep that status quote in place.

Satisfied for the moment, Steve sat down to write a report for the AC and the CC. Before he had hardly started, the sound of incoming choppers brought him to his feet again. He went outside to join AL and Lt Bowes ready to greet the incoming troops. When all the bodies and equipment was unloaded, an Army Major came up to where Steve and co were standing and said, "I am looking for a Detective Chief Superintended Benson."

Séan Louis Moreau had bee carefully siphoning off not only raw diamonds but some of the profits as well. He would guard his little empire with any means available, including the murder of any family members like Gregory, who got too close. What he did not know was that his activities would bring DCS Benson and his small team of investigators into the picture. Steve and his team who were now on his tail, who would find the answers to nail his hide to the barn door. However, for now he went on his merry way building a considerable fortune for when he pulled the plug. His confident grew because he believed he had escape plans to cover any contingency.

So as not to give too much away, Jimmy said, "Two Bears calling. We require both seniors here with additional help in numbers. Have found what we were looking for. Opposition numbers are unknown. Will stand by our current position and wait for your arrival, we are at main grid square 25," Two Bears out.

So nothing wet over the air, Steve said, "These are either the remains of the person we are looking for, or another unsolved murder that has escaped detection," Steve told him.

So standing in front of the newly cleaned whiteboards and waiting until the room had settled before starting. Steve said, "We came out smelling of roses, on our last run-in with the legal profession, but don't let that go to your head. The trouble is we have set the bar very high now, and if we are not careful, we will hang ourselves with our own hype. When we get around to questioning the lead investigators, I will take the DCI, and just for a change, Jimmy can have the DI. If Jimmy gets into trouble, you ca take over Al."

So, after a day Jimmy gave up and returned to the gravesite. By then Donna was ready to return with the remains to the base camp. Jimmy decided to wait until the morning before returning to base. A wise move as there were snow flurries for a time, which would have made traveling very difficult. With a fire going at the mouth of the mineshaft, they stayed warm and dry.

Some of the more level headed members of the crime syndicate wanted Stains roughed up and given his marching orders out of the N WT. However, the hot heads had their way, and Stains life was terminated. This action was not going to let them off the hook as they soon found once Benson was on their trail. By killing Stains, the outcome of their action was the fact that because Stains was a Member of the Current Government that the authorities would not give up the search. Once that happened they would find out quickly enough that Benson and his team did out give up either.

Some time before this, the Politician Gregory Stains arrived in Wrigley on the second half of his official visit on behalf of the Mister for First Nations Affairs. There had bee several incidents involving Members of First Nations and prospectors over land claims due to finding rare minerals particularly diamonds and gold in small deposits, on land that was the sole property of the local First Nations.

Someday,

Stains had an appointment the first Day with Tom Reyolds who was the owner of a small supply business and a licensed assay office. Although Reynolds and several prominent citizens waited a couple of hours for Stains, he was a no-show. Stains was hopeful of gaining a better insight into what his uncle was involved in.

Steve acknowledged with a return salute and shook the Major's had. "This is my 2IC Detective Inspector Al Philips. As the two men shook hads Steve said to Al; "I'm taking the Major inside for an in-depth talk, keep everybody outside and working." Steve followed with; "There is one other of my staff I would like to introduce Detective Sergeant Jimmy Two Bears, a First Nations Tribal Chief, and a wilderness survival expert."

Steve addressing the chopper pilot made sure that once in the air he was to follow any instructions given by Jimmy as long as the safety of the aircraft was not compromised. Around dawn, the following morning the chopper took off with machine gunners riding shotgun on both sides of the helicopter. It followed the path that

Jimmy would have taken on foot in a northeast direction. Jimmy asked the pilot to fly higher and slower so he could more easily read the sign in the snow.

Steve and Al left for the short trip to the barracks. On arrival, they were escorted to the office of the commander Bill Paxton. After introductions, the local chief said, "I was looking forward to meeting you DCS." Steve then gave the commander a quick precis of the case.

Steve Benson could now resume the action to have Moreau and his team of cutthroats put away for the rest of their natural lives. Once Steve having received the message from Jerry Armstrong, and starting from that point, Steve divided the area into grid squares. "Now we know what the plot is," he said to Al, "Let's sit down in a quiet corner and check this grid square on the map. The particular square umber 14 is to the northeast one-third the way out of Wrigley going to Keller Lake. It should only take about thirty minutes to get there. Better still saddle up, we'll head for there now." Over the air, Steve said. "A general message to all units from #1, I will be at grid square 14 if you are need to contact me." Then Steve and Al left to catch up with whatever object had been found at grid square 14.

Steve Benson had been busy having rounded up the fifteen of the attackers and having them shipped back to the RCMP barracks in Wrigley, and guarded by the Canadian Rangers. They would be held there until arrangements were made to send them back to the RCMP HQ for interrogation and charging before being indicted under whatever law covered their recent activities.

Steve called for the senior officer left in charge. His first question was, "Do your choppers carry rockets?"

Steve called in the Major for a conference on where they stood now. "First thing have you got a body count from the mine?"

Steve called Jerry and told him he would standby until Jerry got the AC. With the AC on-air, Steve asked him to return his call on a secure police lie. When the AC called, Steve first gave him a full report before asking him to have Jerry Armstrong search the history of Joe Thompson. "The reason I asked for a secure lie was that I didn't want anyone hearing this. It appears that Thompson was the mastermind behind these attacks. Therefore, the sooner we take Thompson out of the equation, the better. We need to know what connection there is between Thompson and Moreau. Just give Jerry the name and let him work his magic, there is no need to look over his shoulder."

Steve called the base to check on them. It was one of the troopers who answered. Without wasting time or words, Steve told the RCMP trooper that they had come under attack, to batten down the hatches, and be more vigilant. "Pass the word to Jill to leave the computer work for ow just dig in and be ready to defend yourselves in case you come under attack." Steve the put out a general call to have another trooper join Jill just in case.

Steve called the others to take a couple of snowmobiles and trailers to carry the prisoners back to base. At the base camp, one of the men had erected a tent with no sides. The attackers when they arrived were dumped around the central tent pole where everyone could keep an eye on them.

Steve crouched in the middle of the room and got everyone's attention. "I want at least two volunteers to take the fight up to the opposition. The idea is to exit the building quietly and unobtrusively to try and outflank the opposition." All three Jack Armstrong, Jim Henry, and Joe Bascal were the first to put up there hads. To Al Philips, Steve said, "You hold the fort while Jimmy, Jack, Joe and I sneak out to take up the fight. Al, Look for some ribbon or tape to use as armbands, then the rest of you should be able to recognize us in the field. All set up with different armbands Steve gave them the last plan of attack before going out a rear window that was out of view of the attackers under a rock overhang. They moved out in a wide arc before moving in towards the attacker's positions. They took out four of the opposition before the opposition realized they were under attack from the rear.

Steve got hold of Jimmy for a quick talk. "There is no evidence of accommodation, question, where did they live? I want you and Stephens to take one chopper up and fly the surrounding land to look for log cabins or tents. They may be well camouflaged, but hopefully, you will recognize their shape from the air." To the pilot, Steve said, "Again I want you to fly just out of rifle range. Off you go and take as long as you have fuel if necessary."

Steve got hold of Major Fawkner to come and join him in the barracks. With Fawkner seated opposite him, Steve laid out his idea of setting up a military-style tribunal court in the field to question those men before they were taken off their hads. Steve was determined to try to extract some answers, so when the AC next spoke to him, he might have something useful to report.

Steve got on the radio to Yellowknife to talk to the commandant. When he got an answer, Steve said, 'Good mooring sir, I have captured another nine attackers. I need them uplifted by air to your position for interrogation and charging. We are in a bind at the moment, as we have no place to hold them so ASAP if possible."

Steve got up and fetched two cups of coffee for them before sitting down and giving the Major an in-depth report on the current situation. Steve told Fawkner there was no need to take notes, as he would give him a copy of the report he was seeding to the Canadian CC of the RCMP and the Police Service.

Steve had a small guard ready to receive the prisoners. He would try to interrogate them before they were removed back to the RCMP barracks. Steve did not extract much from the interrogation except the name of their boss Joe Thompson. When he got to the point of going nowhere, he gave up. I must get a message through to Jerry Armstrong back at HQ.

Steve introduced himself and did a quick explanation of what he needed. Forbes told him apart from confirming their identity they did not get much more from the house canvas. This couple had only small credit amounts outstanding. In other words your average law-abiding citizens. The couple did not as far as could be ascertained have any connection to underworld crime figures. The DCI did think it could have been a case of mistaken identity but had no way to prove or disprove this theory.

Steve left Donna to examine the gravesite. Later she told Steve, "this person was male according to the bone structure, about 5.'10iches that corresponds to the description I have of Stains. You brought the files with you so I should be able to do a rough crosscheck here. It may turn out to be inaccurate, as our current position is not ideal. Give me at least fifteen to thirty minutes, and I should be able to make a comparison."

Steve left the Major to talk to his troops while Steve had a word with his team. The campsite was already well underway to being finished. Steve and the Major had agreed that everyone understood the first rule that they look for the point of origin instead of worrying about being under fire. Steve explained that it was Jimmy that had added this twist successfully.

Steve made his way back to the central office. "Alright, you geniuses what cases have you decided to tackle first?"

Steve made some soup for himself while he waited for the team to arrive. The chopper came out of the mist and landed in an open space about a hundred meters from the building. They had the equipment unloaded quickly with all hads chipping in. Therefore, the chopper was on its way again with the loss of only thirty minutes. Steve had coffee brewing, so he let them catch their breath while he brought them up to Date.

Steve made sure it was safe before calling in Dr. Donna Connors to join them, at the main site, to examine the remains. She arrived in fifteen minutes by chopper. He had Rangers form a guard around Donna with strict instructions from Steve what should happen if there is another attack. Donna enlisted the help of a couple of Rangers to uncover the human remains before moving them to the mouth of the tunnel, where there was better light.

Steve made sure that Watson understood the RCMP investigation and the criminal trial of Moreau would have to occur first. The takeover could happen. I would like you under the guidance of the Major to form a guard of your fellow tribes-men to guard the mine site while the rest of us get on with it. The order of the day is to repel all borders to either kill or capture any attackers. Of course, the government would be involved, but as you are First Nations, you should not have much of a problem. Steve thought about it some more before he made a report to the AC.

Steve picked up the radio, "Base One to chopper Stand-off, I repeat Stand-off. We are under attack. Report situation to Yellowknife assistance required ASAP. #I out."

Steve pointed the speaker/receiver of his radio clipped to his collar to his mouth. "General message from #1. Sergeant Stephens come and join us at grid square 14 ASAP." To Al, he said, "I'm going to talk to Yellowknife to have them uplift Jimmy and the two ladies here to join us. We need the doc for the remains and Jimmy to have a good look at whatever tracks are left. I am going to leave Jill at the base to be the contact with Jerry and to man the radio, as the listening post."

Steve said, "Benson sir, this will save me the trouble of another phone call." Steve the described the attacks on the group by persons unknown. "Result two bad guys downed and no casualties on our side."

Steve sat in the Wrigley RCMP Post waiting to hear from Donna. He had already told her to take her time as they had plenty now. It was the second day when rifle fire could be heard from outside the building.

Steve the joined Al Philips to discuss the progress so far. They kicked it around for the better part of half an hour before giving it up. "I have to let Jimmy have his head. He will not take kindly to too much interference from me or from the system. Overall, I am pleased we have made some progress. We had nothing to start with, so I believe we have come a long way forward." However, then again this could be dreaming, Steve thought. "I'm going to talk to Jerry to find out how his end is holding up."

Steve then called Al Philips to find out how things were progressing. Al reported that the light snowstorm had stopped, but he had formed a Brach roof over the site anyway.

Steve then called Al, to let him know they were heading back to the gravesite, and to have him send Trooper Armstrong and snowmobile back to the Wrigley base as a backup for Jill. Steve got on air again, "I wat one more trooper who is close to base to report here ASAP." When Armstrong arrived, there would be three RCMP at the base, Trooper Armstrong, one more trooper, and Jill. With the two highly experienced Troopers, they should be able to defend themselves.

Steve thought he could have enjoyed retirement. He did not have any outstanding debts and had enough money I the bank to live I relative comfort. The hard part would be not having a positive direction to help keep his feet planted

Steve thought he would make his report to the AC in the morning. A hearty meal and a good sleep was what he needed. Next morning he made a verbal report to the AC. "Well done," the AC told him, "Were does that leave us?"

Steve thought it was time to have a couple of days to relax. He found out that one of the Rangers was a local tribal chief. He had the Major bring the officer in for a talk. The Ranger volunteer Tom Watson was in fact a local tribal headman and member of the tribal council. With the Major in attendance, it made it easier for Steve to explain the situation. The fact that the local First Nations could take control of the mine. When Steve was sure that Watson understood the situation, he told him to report everything to his tribal council, but to wait until Steve, or his political masters, gave him the word to do anything.

Steve told the sergeant to set up a perimeter guard, as soon as he made the introductions. The sergeant through being part of the survival course run by Jimmy was pleased that they had Jimmy Two Bears on their side. Steve noted that there was a certain amount of rapport between the two. Steve then took the time to find out how the Wrigley base camp was doing.

Steve told the trooper to return to the fork in the trail to act as a guard, just in case.

Steve told them he would give Armstrong fifteen minutes to arrive at the base before they left. He did not wat to leave Jill in a position where she could not defend herself. As soon as the trooper arrived, Steve gave him instructions about setting up a perimeter guard around the base. With the base now more secure, he told the rest to head out for grid square 14. Steve was happier that experienced troopers were making Jill's position safer now they were guarding the station. She was a female officer of the RCMP and should be competent enough to protect herself, but that still does not mean she should be left without protection. Now with extra RCMP troopers, she would be able to concentrate on being logged into their system, and act as their radio listening post.

Steve turned to the Major, "How long do you think we would need to go the distance in the present conditions."

Steve waited for Jimmy to report before his next task to bring the AC up to Date. Steve sat and pulled his thoughts together before he called the AC. Steve knew that this whole situation could get out of had if their political bosses got involved, and tried to stop any more investigation. None the less, he gave the AC a full report on the problem.

Steve went to the front of the whiteboards again. When he had their attention, he said, "Jerry I want you to talk to the parliamentary office that Gregory Stains was attached to at the time, and try to get some idea from the legislative records of Stains' itinerary on the fateful trip. See if you can unearth the possible connection between

Stains ad Reynolds, outside of the usual business commitments. Al, Jill, and Jimmy, you start doing a breakdown of the investigation into the death of the young couple. Donna if you could do your study of the forensic reports such as they are and try to give us some direction."

That is the trouble with some people they have no sense of humour, Steve thought.

The Adams were surprised at how much security the mine had. Unfortunately, they ventured to close to the mine and came under the eye of the mine defenders. There was no hesitation the order was given to have them killed and buried in a remote area. Even Gregory Stains could not help them because by then, he had already been disposed of. Their equipment including their radio was scattered over a large area. The chance of anyone finding the Adam's gear was very small.

The AL spoke up. "I have shortlisted two possible cases. The first being the death of a junior Politician, named Gregory Stains. He had been a politician for only three years but had been bright enough to get himself appointed to a seat on his party's cabinet, and therefore there was a certain amount of initial panic when he disappeared. According to a parliamentary notice, Stains wet to the Territories on a trip around his constituents. One of his functions was as assistant to the minister for Aboriginal affairs, so this particular trip was a fact-finding mission.

The best thing was that there were on local settlements in the vicinity, so their activities went unnoticed. All the heavy machinery required was brought in by chopper in its component parts and assembled on site. The area was mostly wilderness, so getting rid of any spoil from the mine was too difficult. Thompson made sure that the miners were well paid, as his way of keeping them under control.

The chopper in question was a modern all-weather executive machine, with a fully enclosed passenger cabin. Thompson also had a license to fly the machine, so between the two of them they should be able to get themselves out of any trouble they might encounter. When the pilot arrived, Grace told him to go straight in.

The chopper put down onto the snow very gently so as not to disturb any sign on the ground. Jimmy and the sergeant were dressed in arctic survival clothing, and as both were seasoned winter experts, they could not or should not get into any trouble, besides they could always call the chopper for a pickup. They separated with about 50 meters between them and did a slow march alongside what was an indistinct trail. They carried on for about five klms before Jimmy called a halt. The chopper had taken off and was shadowing them just out of rifle range. Jimmy put his arm up and pointed in the general direction he thought the bad guys had gone and said into his radio, "Air one go out in this general direction," he said, pointing with his arm, "For about 15 klms and have a look-see and report. We will follow on foot. Then you can come back and pick us up."

The chopper, which was not armed showed good judgment; stood-off just out of rifle rage, just as the radio spoke, "Commander, Yellowknife, report your situation and casualty umbers."

The choppers proceeded to attack with greater vigour. I no time due to the opposition sustaining heavy casualties they grounded their weapons and surrendered. Steve called the senior military officer to send in the vehicles to pick up the bodies, while the walking wounded were frog-marched out of the area as well to where they would be picked up later and taken to a detention centre already set up for the purpose.

The commander in Yellowknife put an urgent call out for the Chief Commissioner. Once he had him on air, he quickly gave a report and put a demand in for some help from the military. The CC told him to stand fast while he started organizing heavy weapons. "Directly attacking our system of law and order has to stop before every lowlife in Canada thinks they can declare war on the RCMP." He made that point forcefully when he spoke directly to the General commanding the multi-purpose gunship units. The general then spoke directly with Commander Paxton in Yellowknife, at the same time he was instructing his Flag Officer which group to launch. By the end of the phone call, four Blackhawk choppers had be deployed. They arrived in short order and did an aerial recon to access the situation.

The couple who were enjoying the wilderness on their honeymoon had chosen the wilderness trip as something different. The couple in question had a permanent home in Edmonton, Alberta. They have been identified as Sean and Sally Adams. They apparently had well-paid steady employment, with no reference to them in the police criminal files. Steve thought about it but had not broached the idea of mistaken identity; he would do it when he talked to Edmonton?

The group that waited that fateful Day for Stains had a list of complaints about the inefficiencies of the State Treasury, as regards the quality of gold ore and rough diamonds. Reynolds could get around the gold by doing ay umber of tests of the metal, but the diamonds were another thig. The diamonds had to be sent to the Capital to be assayed by diamond merchants, and several shipments had gone missing. It had gotten to the point when small business owners like Reynolds could no longer afford the payments for insurance coverage. That was why he and the other business owners needed to have an in-depth talk to Stains, to voice their displeasure with how the government was hadling the whole process.

The Helicopter was one of the latest Sikorsky S-92 all-weather VIP aircraft, generally used by mining companies when prospecting for oil and gas deposits, on one had. On the other had, to fly relief crews to and from oilrigs on the ocean.

The Major gave a smart salute and said, "I'm Major Brian Fawkner Canadian Ranger Corp reporting as ordered, sir."

The Major quickly rounded up Al, Jimmy, and his two best pilots and was airborne within twenty minutes. Once hovering near the site identified by Jimmy, The Major used the loud hailer of the chopper telling anyone in the area to lay down his or her arms and surrender, or be destroyed with the building. He gave them ten minutes, repeated the same message, waited five minutes before giving his pilots the order to fire. Four rockets were launched at the target, resulting in a cloud of snow, rock and building materials being thrown into the air. When the dust settled, the Major had his machine gunners rake the area to discourage anybody on the ground putting up any form of resistance. He ordered his pilots drop him, Jimmy, Al and six Rangers on the ground and told the choppers to hover over the area as their aerial bodyguards.

The Major who was sitting in during Jimmy's debriefing said, "I'll go and organize the chopper now DCS, and bring back the pilot for any more instructions you want to give." The Major went off to get hold of the best chopper pilot who was with the group. After a short talk, they went back to the barracks to report to Steve.

The mine was starting to yield some reasonable quantities of gold, which was even more reason to keep its existence under wraps. It was the first time in life that Moreau had taken up a position in the slow lane because even he realized the enormous potential of the mine. Steve Benson representing the Law of Canada would eventually bring Moreau to stand in front of a judge to be sentenced for his crimes.

The pilot chose the right-had group and continued to fly after them under Jimmy's direction. After another five or six klms, Jimmy lost the sig. To the pilot, he said put down somewhere convenient, the sergeant and I will track it on foot for a time to see if we can pick up the trial."

The problem was that they were in that area of the Northwest Territories, which had yielded Gold strikes and better still, diamonds. Already tall tales were doing the rounds about fallouts between prospectors about who had the legitimate rights to whatever was found.

The process of questioning the opposition was relentless but very little was forthcoming. Steve and the Major had only interviewed two-thirds of the men when the word came that there were three choppers on the way to pick up the prisoners. The only useful thing that Steve had gleamed reading between the lines was there was a mine somewhere in the area that these men were employed to protect. Nevertheless, no one would give a location, or what minerals the mine could have produced. More importantly, who was pulling strings in the background? One thing was evident these men were either gold hard rock miners or oil workers and tough as they come. In other words as a group, they would not crack under cross-examination.

The Rangers were organized quickly, so they were on the move in fifteen minutes. The three groups moved out without making any noise and approached the mine entrance. With the ability to camouflage themselves in the snow, they got to within 100 meters without being challenged. Steve said quietly into his radio mick, "Everybody stand fast while the Major and I have a look see." The two men made a slow approach one to either side of the entrance. Steve thought it strange that no one seemed to be guarding the mine. He was about to stand up when a shot was fired from inside the shaft in his direction.

The report was that everything was quiet now. Steve warned them that they could not afford to relax, that the absence of sound might be the calm before the storm. "Jill you have three experienced officers there make use of them, but none the less ensure you are set up to repel all borders, so protect yourselves at all costs. #1 is listening out."

The sergeant said quietly, "That was well doe, Jimmy." Then the first head popped up from under the snow, soon the whole bunch was exposed and stood with their hads in the air.

The small group from Wrigley (Steve, Jimmy, and Donna) had only gone about 800 hundred meters on the way back to the gravesite when several shots kicked up the snow around the small convoy. The sound of their snowmobiles and the snow covered any noise the rifles would have made when fired. Without hesitation, as the rounds seemed to have come from his right Steve pointed with his left had and moved in that direction deeper into the bush. He wanted to stay within rifle rage of the shooter or shooters. While Jimmy quickly formed a perimeter guard, Steve called Jill to make sure the base was still functioning. Steve was confident their heavy weather outer clothing would camouflage them and make them difficult targets to hit

The two men kicked the problem around for the better part of an hour before a consensual agreement was reached about what would be the order of business, and the flow of information, and importantly the chain of command. Steve already had an extended map of the area spread out on the table. Because Steve was addressing a military commander, he did not have to worry about map coordinates and compass bearings.

The ultimate consequence of his actions would make a solid case for the High Court. That would find that Moreau's actions, including murder of persons known and unknown, plus his Major corporate crime, would stand as proved. The Court would had down a sentence of the death penalty, or a commuted life sentence never to be released. His entire fortune would be confiscated and put into a government account to be used only for humanitarian projects in Canada and Third World Countries, all under Canadian control.

There did not seem to be any doubt which direction the opposition was headed. It looked like the attackers were heading to either Norman Wells or Fort Good Hope, before possibly crossing the county border into Nunavut. Jimmy called the chopper back for a pickup.

There was no sign of anybody at the gravesite until Al Philips poked his head up from under the snow. As there was only the three of them, Al and the sergeant, and one trooper, they could have been in serious trouble if they had come under attack. Therefore, the best thing they could have done was to make themselves into snow bunnies.

There were a couple of clicks before a male voice said, "DCI Bria Forbes."

Therefore, using her skill Donna can hopefully give us an ID using DNA. In addition, Al reports that it has stopped snowing. However, to make sure, I had Al build a temporary roof over the site, which has now been overlaid by a thin layer of snow, making it look like the surrounding bush.

Donna, now we have the other snowmobiles, we will take all of your forensic equipment whether or not we use it.

They came in behind the two choppers on the ground. Jimmy and Stephens were standing by when Steve and the Major disembarked as the helicopter touched the snow. The Rangers quickly demounted and had their equipment sorted and ready to move in minutes. Jimmy spread the map out on the floor of the chopper. He pointed to the possible mine site and stood back so everyone could have a look.

They had covered about fifteen klms when Jimmy asked the pilot to swing around in a full arc. He had the pilot fly the same arc three times before asking him to hover over a particular spot. Into his microphone, he said, "Have a look down now, you can see where the group of attracters has separated into two halves before going in different directions."

To Al, Steve said, "Anyone else leading that little band I might worry, but if I start worrying about Jimmy, it will be time to retire. I'm going to have a word with Yellowknife using the radio from here."

Trooper Jim Henry on air said, "I can head there now. I can be there in ten minutes, boss."

Using a small canvas sack, Jimmy the ordered the attackers to put the rest of their weapons into the bag and to lay down their long guns in the snow. There were nine attackers' altogether, six from under the snow and the three that were already under arrest. One of the men whispered, "We could have taken them," before Jimmy gave him a blow to the back of his head. "That was for thinking that we were a bunch of amateurs." While he had them on the ground, Jimmy cable tied their hads and feet; now they were about to go anywhere

Using the two-way radio, Steve called Jerry back at the office. With the preliminaries over, Steve asked Jerry had he made any progress at all tracking Stains' itinerary.

What Steve would not know at the time was that this was the spot where Stains was murdered and his body put in a shallow grave and covered with loose soil. That was what the trooper had found.

When he got back to the office, Steve called Yellowknife base to warn them, and to ensure that whatever assistance was needed would be extended to the trio if required. He also wanted to make sure that the trio had access to snowmobiles, trailers, and dog sled teams, and most importantly tents and sleeping bags.

When Steve and Al arrived they found two trails lead off into the bush from a corner of the grid square 14. The trooper who called them to this location had his snowmobile hidden from view to conceal his presence when the two officers arrived. As the two officers approached his position, he stepped out from hiding to flag them down.

When Steve came out of his office, Donna said, "I believe that the only way to move forward is to do a foot search of the area with old eagle eyes, Jimmy, to see if we can pick up something that could have been missed. What do you think about that Jimmy?"

When Steve had as much information he was likely to have, he told Al that he was heading back to base to talk to Wrigley. "Al, you hold on here till you hear from me. Maybe you could build a temporary roof over the grave site to keep off as much snow as possible." That left three at the gravesite for security. Steve then left to return to the base camp at Wrigley, satisfied that everything was progressing in the right direction.

When Steve had Yellowknife on air, he asked for the CO. There was no time wasting before the CO came on air. "DCS Benson sir. I will not waste time recalling the events regarding Aylmer Lake. You would be more aware of the situation regarding my people doing an investigation. I have every confidence that DS Two Bears will have it under control. I would like you to put in place an emergency Evac should it become necessary, as my people discovered they have already been under surveillance."

When Steve picked up his phone having been warned by Jerry, he said, "DCS Benson speaking Ma'am, from the cold case squad in Ottawa."

When the group on the ground were satisfied that, all equipment and accommodations had been destroyed the Major had the choppers pick them up to return to base. When Jimmy told him the attack was a success, Steve told him to leave one chopper and half the force as a guard. Steve ordered the Major to return to base, after reporting success to Steve. In the base office, he joined Steve in a Toast to that success, strictly off the record. As it was late, The entire exercise allowing for travel time had only taken three hours, time well spent.

When the trio arrived in Yellowknife, they were picked up by a couple of constables in a small bus and taken to the barracks. The commandant was there to greet them. Jimmy asked the CO if he could have two additional troopers as a backup. As Jimmy told the CO, they would need to have had extreme weather training and be well versed in the use of a long gun.

When the trooper arrived, Steve left Al to grill the RCMP trooper for about fifteen minutes on how or why he found the gravesite. Trooper Joe Bascal stated that he had found a leg bone and some animal tracks leading away. Out of curiosity, Bascal decided to follow them resulting in him finding the gravesite. What made it a bit easier was the fact that the whole search area had been broken down by the use of grid squares. Right from the start, Steve had made it very clear that anyone referring to a particular area when they used the two-way radio, was to put the grid square umber only over the airwaves, hopefully, this would keep the band guys confused.

When they finished their coffee, Jimmy took them to a starting point from where they could examine the area. He put sticks to mark the start, and every time they charged direction. Their routine over the exit two Days was fixed and relentless but they none the less managed to cover a ten sq. klm section. Anything they found was left in place and flagged with a marker, which Jimmy copied to a map of the area, using his portable compass.

While Donna patched up the wounded on both sides, Steve contacted the AC about picking up both the bodies and the injured to clear the site. The opposition wounded would be taken away for interrogation before being charged and tried in a court, if found guilty would eventually be sent to prison.

While he reminisced, there was a knock on the office door before his secretary came in with a fax note in her had.

While Jerry was involved in that Steve, had his own set of problems fighting the bad people. With all the prisoners off his hads, Steve briefed Major Brian Fawkner of the Rangers about what he should do with what Jimmy believed was a building, camouflaged to look like part of the surrounding wilderness. "I would like you to take a couple of choppers with long rage fuel tanks, capable of firing rockets to destroy the structure. You can use a loud hailer to warn anyone hiding to surrender or suffer the consequents of what was about to happen. Take Al and Jimmy with you in case you have to make any arrests. The order of the day is 'total destruction of whatever is there. I would like you to leave now.'"

While Steve thought about that, the AC John Seymour, made an entrance, "Good morning all. I came to welcome Jerry back into the fold. The CC also extends his good wishes."

While they were waiting, the two senior men went over the plan again to make sure nothing had been missed. As soon as Stephens reported back, Steve, the Major, and Stephens left to go the Ranger HQ's tent. The extra Mounties had already reported to the Ranger HQ, where they were standing by waiting for further orders. Steve wanted to say a few words to his men as well as the Rangers to impress on them the importance of what they were doing. He also wanted to impress on them that where possible to try to keep as many of the opposition alive. "Remember," he told them, "You cannot use dead bodies in a courtroom to point out the accused. At the same time, I am not sending you out, to sacrifice your lives for the cause. Your safety is paramount in a shootout, beyond that I am too concerned, as long as it is not you in the body bag. In other words, do not take unnecessary risks."

With everyone kitted out they were more or less ready for the off. That was when Steve got the disturbing news from Jimmy, who was approximately in the same area as Aylmer Lake.

With everything underway, Steve called his boss the AC. Steve said hello and then gave a comprehensive report on what occurred.

With Jerry back on the lie, Steve first asked if his conversation with the AC bee recorded.

With that said, Steve gave the DCI his number and asked that he be contacted immediately if Edmonton made any breakthroughs

With the camp strategically guarded by concealed sub-machine guns mounted on 360-degree tripods, everything was set with a siege in mind. With everyone settled in, the campsite was quiet for two days until the evening of the second day, when they came under direct attack from the east quarter, around seven thirty in the evening. It was not so much the bad people doing the shooting, as the return fire from the sub-machine guns that grabbed everyone's attention.

With the Commandant on air, Steve did not waste any time. 'Benson here sir. We have found another gravesite here in the approximate area where the person we are looking for went missing. I need my pathologist Dr. Connors, and Jimmy Two Bears here now. Can you have my three individuals and their equipment uplifted by air to Wrigley immediately? It is snowing in the area where the grave site is located, so the sooner I can have the team here the better."

With the snowmobile engines shut down, an uneasy calm settled over the small group. Two more rounds kicked up snow to their right side front. Jimmy, as usual, was waiting and fired two shots at their point of origin to be rewarded when they heard one of the opposition shout as if he might have been hit, followed by the sound of two snowmobiles starting up their engines. Jimmy fired four more rounds in that direction just to make sure the bad guys were vacating the area. The sound quickly died as the snow machines moved away.

With the three troopers, that Steve had sent to cover the base, and with himself, Al, Jill, Jimmy, the sergeant and 2 more constables, they had a strength of ten to protect the outpost. Steve had the sergeant draw up a schedule for a perimeter guard. Once done Steve could now relax and focus on trying to find out whose remains they had found.

With their overnight bags which Steve made a rule be kept in the HQ, Steve accompanied them to the airport with the usual warnings about keeping their heads down and following Jimmy's directions if the weather closed in. Steve told them to take their time, especially as they had plenty of that now. Lastly, He said to them that he would make sure they had plenty of backup from Yellowknife.

With tongue I cheek, I asked, "Does this mean sir; our hard and mostly unrewarded efforts have made you look good to the CC." Steve wanted to know.

"The remains of two bodies of a young male and female have been discovered by a party of campers about 48 kilometres south of Aylmer Lake. As it happens, I was on a family camping and fishing trip to the area. The area is northeast of Yellowknife, and south of Aylmer Lake in the Northwest Territories. The area where the remains were found was off the beaten track and would have gone undiscovered for a very long time. The difficulty is access to this section of the wilderness, for police conducting an in-depth investigation, as the small township of Reliance is the nearest point to civilization."

CPSIA information can be obtained
at www.ICGtesting.com
Printed in the USA
BVHW071639290519
549569BV00004B/379/P